ALSO BY DENNIS PATRICK MURPHY

The Thin Blue Line Series

CPD Blue—True Crime: The Rookie Years #1

SPD Blue—True Crime: Urban Policing #2

SPD Blue—True Crime: Narcotics #3

SPD Blue - True Crime: Sex Crimes #4

SPD Blue—True Crime: Major Crimes #5

The Thin Blue Line Series #6

DENNIS MURPHY

SPD BLUE

TRUE CRIME

SPECIAL AGENT

SPD Blue—True Crime: Special Agent
THE THIN BLUE LINE SERIES #6

This book is a work of fiction. Characters, corporations, institutions, and organizations in this novel are the author's imagination, or if real, are used fictitiously without any intent to describe their actual content.

For information, contact:
THE THIN BLUE LINE SERIES
http://www.thethinbluelineseries.com

ISBN: 9798218638801
First Edition: July 2024
10 9 8 7 6 5 4 3 2 1

SPD BLUE

TRUE CRIME

THE THIN BLUE LINE SERIES #6

<u>SPECIAL AGENT</u>

A NOVEL

DENNIS PATRICK MURPHY

I dedicate this novel to the men and women I honorably served with in the United States Navy and the United States Air Force; and all the other service men and women who are currently serving, have served, or have given their lives in the defense of this great country.

Fair winds and following seas...

In memorial to the late - Carol Ann Murphy - Mother, Confidant, Friend: This will be all that much harder without your constant encouragement and guidance throughout the writing process. Eternally grateful and forever mournful.

- *Your eldest son.*

SPD BLUE

FOREWORD

The beating he was taking was unsustainable. Every time Mac delivered a punch to the assailant, he took two blows to the back of his head from the pair of gang bangers behind him. His knees buckled after every hit, but he was determined to stay in the fight and hold the third man against the parked car and keep swinging.

Adding to the complexity of the situation, Mac's left foot was tightly wrapped up in ace bandages. Not long ago, he was gripping his steel crutches, feeling the cold metal against his palms as he moved around the Armory Square business district in downtown Syracuse.

Initially, the third man Mac was engaged with had attacked him fiercely. Now, however, he was content to just parry Mac's strikes and let his allies on the back side do their worst.

As the melee raged on, Mac felt a cold snowflake land on his eyelash, its crystalline beauty standing out amongst the chaos. He could sense it melting, as dark clouds in his head swirled and his legs continued to rachet his body down into the cold slushy snow beneath him in the street. The punches from behind kept coming as Mac was being dragged away from the present...

CHAPTER ONE

It had been four years since Mac had first been assigned to the Criminal Investigations Division of the City of Syracuse Police Department. The winds of change had blown other members into and out of Major Crimes, as it was commonly known.

Sure, the stalwart detectives were solving crimes, as they had when Mac first started with the unit back in 1998; but a new group of cops were always on the heels of the old.

Captain Richard Walsh was still running the show, and the rather popular Lieutenant Shelby Steele was ever-present as the executive officer. Detective Sergeant Bruce Merrill and Detective Sergeant Corey Barlow were still the first-line bosses on the evening shift, referred to as the Third Platoon.

Mac had spent most of his time on the Third Platoon in CID, with only a brief respite to the day shift, known as Second Platoon.

CID Second Platoon perpetually had the fewest changes in the division. Once a detective made it to the 0800 hours–1600 shift, they were set for the rest of their career. There were very few positions within SPD where you could be a DT working the dayshift.

So, that is where one would find the lifers in the police department–the detectives with over thirty years of aggregate service. Most cops left when they reached their twentieth year to collect half of their salary before starting another career someplace else with that in their back pocket.

But the day DTs knew they had a good thing and were content to ride out their days carrying a gold shield and being at the top of the heap at SPD.

Maximum civil service age for being a cop in New York State was sixty-two years old. The resolute pair of Potts and Kettles were pushing forty years of police service and rapidly coming up on the magic number. Bob "Ace" Murray and his partner, Mike "Cement Head" Macko, had been On the Job since the early seventies; and they weren't leaving until they were forced out the door.

The affable detectives were largely built and imposing; complete with square jaws and broken noses. Their wardrobe was straight out of the late seventies, with plaid sports coats, wide dress pants, and black oxford shoes. The pair resembled leg breakers for mobsters years ago, but were the most entertaining DTs assigned to CID.

And, once again, they were holding court at the end of their shift, with the younger detectives assigned to the Third Platoon as their raptured but skeptical audience.

"So, these two niner white guys on the south side are roomies. They were drinking Boone's Farm wine and smoking hash; when apparently, they started to disagree," Ace Murray had started to say to a packed room in the bullpen.

"What's a niner?" One of the fairly new DTs named Lou asked. He didn't have that much time On the Job or as a detective.

"It's from back in the day when the department ran two-number patrol car designations for the territories. It was on the westside in the 59 section, which became terminology for the hapless citizenry that resided there. The 59 term was shortened to 9'er," Mike Macko helpfully explained.

"Oh," said the new DT.

"Thank you, Cement Head. Anyway, these two-half fucked-up niners start going at it, for only God knows what, when one of them pulls a Samurai sword off the mantle over the dilapidated fireplace and goes after his roommate," Ace continued.

Mostly silence in the third-floor bullpen of the Criminal Investigations Division in the headquarters' building of SPD. Ace Murray's cigarette smoke swirled and mixed with the ever-present stale coffee smell within the room. He flicked ashes from his cigarette into an old copper ashtray on the corner of his desk as he spoke.

The constant muted police chatter could be heard from the turned down portable radios of the DTs that sat on the corner of their desks.

"This can't be good," Zachary Fry said, sitting straighter in his office chair.

"Not for the roommate." Macko added.

"How many times did he dice him?" Liam Fletcher asked.

Ace just smiled, taking another pull off his cigarette as he watched the red glowing embers fully ignite once more.

Macko couldn't help himself, "Just once."

"Only once? Did he lop his head off?" Perla "Pocahontas" Hamilton inquired, putting down the file she had in her hand.

"Nope. He just impaled him," Ace answered, taking his time to distill the story to his eager audience of junior detectives.

"He just stabbed him?! I thought this was some kind of gruesome assault?" Waldon West said what everybody else was thinking in the bullpen. Waldon was working on his own cig, with his cowboy boots up on the corner of his desk.

"It's how he did it, folks. Go ahead Ace, tell the naysayers." Macko again nudged the story along.

Ace smiled thinly as he delivered the coup de grâce, "The bad guy impaled the three-foot Katana sword into his right shoulder to the hilt, at an angle, and the point of the sword came out his left lower back."

"Holy shit! Was he DRT?" Asked Tabitha Cherry.

"What's DRT?" Lou asked again, confused.

"Well, you've heard of DOA, which means Dead on Arrival, right?" Macko obligingly said.

Lou just nodded up and down.

"DRT means, Dead Right There."

Lou thought about it a moment and then got a gleam in his eye, "Oh."

"That's an unofficial term kid. Don't put that in any

of your CID reports," Macko followed up.

"Any way, the vic's not dead. Not even close. The path of the sword missed all vital organs. Just some minor internal bleeding," Ace finished up the tale, extinguishing his spent cigarette into the copper ashtray. He calmly looked at all the assembled DTs, waiting for the debate to start, which he knew it most certainly would.

"How is that possible?" Ian Atkinson asked, looking at his fellow DTs.

"I'm definitely calling bullshit on that!" Zach interjected.

"Yeah Ace, I think you finally got caught telling a fib this time," Tabitha said, smiling at the old gumshoe.

"That dog won't hunt," said Waldon, as he took his boots off his desk and went back to his stack of reports.

Potts and Kettles just smiled at each other, letting the debate rage on.

"Come on Ace, you know, that does seem a little too far-fetched for a bunch of cops to believe," Mac finally waded in on the tale.

The old-time partners continued with the mischievous looks until Ace said, "Go ahead Cement Head, show them."

Macko reached into the inside pocket of his plaid sports coat with his sausage sized fingers producing a polaroid picture. He held up the photo between his oversized fingers; featuring a camera angle of the victim from behind. The vic was standing in a hospital trauma room, naked from the waist up.

All the DTs got out of their desk chairs for a closer look at the snapshot.

Sure enough, there it was. The elaborate decorated handle of the Katana sword sticking out of the roommate's right shoulder, and the glistening silver colored point of the sword—dripping with blood—sticking out of the left portion of his lower back.

"No fuckin way!" Zach squealed.

"Oh my God!" Pocahontas replied in return.

"Holy shit!" Waldon breathed out, putting his cases back down.

"Another one for the books, Ace," Tabitha said, a

little embarrassed she doubted the oracle of cop stories.

Ace and Macko took in the acknowledgment with stride. They knew exactly how they had played the room and it ended just the way they knew it would.

Ace stood up and put on his own plaid sports coat. "It's time for me and my friend to get out of here and get a short one. Coleman's?"

"Well, I don't mind if we do," Macko answered as always.

It was a typical change of shift in Major Crimes. The day shift leaving and the Third Platoon getting ready for the busiest tour in CID.

The evening detectives never knew what the city would throw at them from night to night, but it was nice to have camaraderie and the boisterous banter from the old timers before shit got real.

Even though Mac was lamenting being left behind in Major Crimes by his good friends that had been promoted to sergeant; he still enjoyed being in the whirlwind of CID.

He and his fellow DTs were always working the most

high-profile investigations in the City of Syracuse. If it was newsworthy, you would find the detectives in Major Crimes in the bullpen, on the third floor, within Syracuse Police Department headquarters working the case.

It was all Mac really wanted when he transferred here twelve years ago from his small hometown PD, but with time comes growth. He had enough time and experience to become a boss like his friends; but he was still sitting third on the promotional list, which was dragging on for who knew how long.

But, at this very moment, he enjoyed the camaraderie between the DTs in CID, with their shared laughter and conversations echoing throughout the hallowed chamber of major crime investigations.

"Success is not the key to happiness. Happiness is the key to success. If you love what you are doing, you will be successful."

- Albert Schweitzer

CHAPTER TWO

Patrick "Mac" MacKenna was a six foot, broad-shouldered, brown-haired, forty-year-old single father of three children from his first marriage. After nine years of raising them practically by himself, the kids were all out of the house.

Bridget had started community college, but then decided to live with Mac's youngest sister in Florida. Joseph was in his sophomore year at Utica College at Syracuse University, majoring in Economic Crime Investigation. And most disheartening to Mac, his youngest, Elizabeth, had moved back in with her mother.

He was estranged from his second wife, NMI, over the issue of the children. She wanted her own, and Mac was treading water on just taking care of the three he had. They still loved each other and saw each other from time to time, but the nine years apart—and dating other people - had taken a toll on their once Irish fairytale romance.

Although, NMI took care of the house and Guinness the dog when he was called up for military service after 9/11. Mac had come off active duty in July and NMI had gone back to the house she grew up in to live with her father.

So, at the moment, Mac lived alone in the small white Cape Cod house. It was on an acre and a half of land surrounded by a white picket fence, across from Pine Grove Golf Course & Fitness Center, located in the Town of Camillus. He wasn't totally alone, as he had Guinness, the dog. The Black Labrador Rottweiler mix was indeed his best friend. He spent hours talking to the kind and gentle bearlike pet when he was at the homestead.

Mac had wed young. Marrying his high school sweetheart shortly after he started college because of her becoming pregnant with Bridget. He was relegated to dropping out of college and working three minimum wage jobs at the same time just to get by.

Eventually, his first wife continued to get pregnant with Joseph and Elizabeth, with a miscarriage in between, that unceremoniously ended the marriage. Mac hadn't been involved with the family planning and found himself working all the time and seldom got to spend time with his kids.

When he was younger, he briefly thought about being a priest, but after the advent of his high school girlfriend, that changed his direction to work in law enforcement as a cop. For Mac, it was all about the good versus evil thing.

When he turned twenty-one, Mac was able to get his New York State pistol permit and went to work for an all-African American security company in the inner city of Syracuse. He was doing low-income housing security work at Hill Top apartments on the eastside of the city. Within a short time, because of his managerial skills he learned working for his father in the hospitality business, the African-American owner asked Mac to run the security company.

He parlayed this into becoming a police officer for his hometown—the Town of Camillus—when Mac turned twenty-three years old. Just about five years later, he was able to laterally transfer over to the City of Syracuse Police Department as a cop.

As a city copper, he went back to the Hill Top Apartment complex and worked a walking beat for two years; making mostly gun and drug arrest. That got him transferred to Narcotics within the Special Investigations Division. There he worked Anti-Crime for two years; before going undercover for the Central New York Drug Enforcement Administration Task Force as a principal undercover operative.

Mac loved drug work, but had a falling out with his untrained SPD narcotics supervisor at the DEA Task Force: finding himself back on Road Patrol for the City of Syracuse after the yearlong undercover assignment. Back in uniform, he pushed a marked car around on Third Platoon for about a year answering 911 dispatched calls for service in the city, before being offered a detective position in the newly formed Abused Persons Unit. This investigatory unit examined all sex crime cases, which unfortunately mostly involved young children.

After exactly a year, Mac was able to transfer as a detective to the Criminal Investigations Division. He liked working Major Crimes, but Mac was getting burned out after four years.

All his good friends On the Job: Francis Tucker, Kylen "Hammer" Duffy, Roderick Dalton, Scott Sutton, Tatum Fuller, Gil Lockhart - mostly from investigations - had all been promoted, but Mac was still sitting third on the sergeant's list because of a hiring freeze.

That being what it was, Mac had just finished up lifting free weights and doing a bunch of cardio over at Pine Grove Fitness Center. His house was eerily quiet without his children in it, and it weighed on him. Guinness, the dog, was looking sad as well, not having the kids to interact with.

Taking a shower, Mac changed into a Brooks Brothers green corduroy sports coat, blue poplin button down collared dress shirt, a brown chestnut colored tie, khaki colored dress pants, and tan Johnston & Murphy plain toe oxford laced up shoes.

Fall could be fickle in Central New York and the corduroy coat fit the bill for this evening's tour in Major Crimes.

Making sure Guinness had full bowls of water and food; Mac scratched his anvil sized head before leaving out the back door heading for the unattached double garage on the side of his home.

Because he was now alone, Mac sold the emerald green Chevy Blazer he once chauffeured the children around in, and bought an older, midnight black, Porsche 924 S. It wasn't a 911, but on Mac's meager budget, it would do nicely for a unique German sports car.

He found the Bavarian machine parked in the garage next to his black 1999 Harley Davidson 883 Sportster motorcycle that he had bought new. This was the most extravagant purchase he had ever made. Acquired four years earlier, it gave him a mode of transportation to the PD, allowing his older children access to the family car for school and extracurricular activities. The Porsche was impractical for the Central New York weather, but it made Mac feel less empty.

His inner voice interjected. "Mid-life crisis is what it is!"

Mac's inner voice had many opinions, although, at times, they were undoubtedly warranted.

The Porsche sprang to life as Mac turned the key. He left the shelter of the garage for the short ten-minute ride from the country setting to the City of Syracuse Police Headquarters.

*

SPD Headquarters, located at 511 South State Street in downtown Syracuse, had been there since 1964. Situated within the Public Safety Building, the Police Front Desk was found on the first floor as you entered the building. Some citizens would walk in to report crimes that weren't called in to the 911 Dispatch Center.

The Records Division is on the second floor. Citizens would retrieve police reports from this location.

The Criminal Investigations Division is positioned on the third floor. Major Crimes was perpetually busy and both cops and civilians were seen coming and going at all hours.

The fourth floor contained the Chief of Police, Deputy Chiefs, and all the other police administration staff that went along with it.

Training Division, including the Syracuse Police Academy, is housed on the fifth floor of the PSB.

The fifth floor also had a complete gymnasium where the cops did in-service Defensive Tactics training and played pickup basketball on their off time.

The City of Syracuse Fire Department occupied the sixth floor. Naturally, they had firehouses all over the city, but the command staff had their administrative offices in this part of the building.

The basement contained the Police Pistol Range, a couple of workout rooms with free weights and cardio machines, with separate locker rooms for the men and women of the Syracuse Police Department.

Of course, there were other smaller units within the

divisions that were scattered around inside of the PSB; but these were the main units and spaces in the City of Syracuse Police Department.

The Police Garage and Uniform Division Roll Call had moved to 2109 Erie Boulevard East, along with other locker rooms for the Road Patrol cops.

Special Investigations Division was located at a secret off-site location. It was the Bat Cave for narco, vice, and tech ops detectives.

Mac was entering his seventeenth year of his law enforcement career, but the PSB was home. The facility was showing its age and the two elevators seemed to have minds of their own, but he couldn't imagine working anyplace else.

This was one of those buildings that a person would think of when they'd hear, "If walls could talk..."

The history here comes and goes with each cohort of cops. But Mac figured most of it was lost in those transitions. There was just too much of it to retain and the constant generational turnover, one after another, just kept coming.

As Mac walked into the PSB to start the evening shift, he nodded at the Desk Sergeant as he pushed the UP button, waiting for the wayward elevator; his mind wandered as to what untold stories surely lay within these ancient granite walls. Maybe, just maybe, another detective just starting the evening shift in the late sixties or seventies wondered the same thing.

Mac adjusted his tie as he let this idea take shape in his head, letting himself be amused at the mere contemplation of it.

The law isn't justice. It's a very imperfect mechanism. If you press exactly the right buttons and are also lucky, justice may show up in the answer. A mechanism is all the law was ever intended to be.

- Raymond Chandler

CHAPTER THREE

The human form that used to be a person just minutes earlier, was splayed out in the front yard of 1616 East Fayette Street. The two-story chestnut-colored clapboard-sided structure loomed over the body. Neighbors and passersby alike gathered just outside the all too familiar yellow crime scene tape that cordoned off the area around the run-down edifice.

Mac didn't have time to consider his musings over what longtime ago detectives had thought or not. The homicide had been called into CID just before the 1600 hours start time for the Third Platoon detectives, and the DTs had been promptly sent out to the scene to detect.

The dilapidated two-family house within the crime scene tape sat up off the street on a little knoll; separated from the road by the pale gray pockmarked sidewalk that passed in front of the death scene. Candy wrappers, amber-colored forty-ounce beer bottles, and hollowed-out cigar shavings littered the front yard with untold other rubbish next to the soulless body.

The late day autumn sun filtered through an old sycamore tree planted on the property in more prosperous days. The scent of the overworked sewers from the nearby Hill Top Apartment complex wafted down on onlookers and cops alike.

Uniformed patrol coppers were dotted along the fluttering crime scene tape as Mac ducked under. Heading up the slight grade of the steps that led to the front porch; he offered a slight glance over to the corpse that had come to land just off the left side of the wooden stairway.

Detective Sergeant Corey Barlow was speaking with a uniformed sergeant, who was giving him the down-low on what had occurred before the DT's arrival.

Barlow was known as 'Ironside's' among the ornerier detectives on the Third Platoon. It was an unflattering moniker and a nod to a television crime drama from the late sixties to the mid-seventies that featured Raymond Burr as Robert T. Ironside. A consultant for the San Francisco Police Department, who was paralyzed from the waist down and was consigned to life in a wheelchair.

Detective Sergeant Barlow had spent quite a few years in Major Crimes. First as a detective and now as a boss. The six-foot one-inch frame, salt and peppered hair of a Barlow was stooped over a slight pot belly on pin legs. The bespectacled supervisor had achieved the monicker from his DTs, not because of an ailment, but because he barely left the office.

The Job had gotten to Barlow, but he did his best when it came to running homicide scenes.

"Hey Mac! Help Fletcher and Fry interview the family," Barlow said as he continued his conversation with the uniformed sergeant.

Mac nodded and kept on walking into the dwelling. Wailing could be heard from somewhere inside the first floor of the two-family structure.

Liam Fletcher was a tall, thin redhead who had a passion for all things Jimmy Buffett. He had been a transfer from a small town outside the City of Syracuse just like Mac.

Zachariah Fry was also a transfer from a village PD just outside the city. He had a diminutive stature, but had become a martial arts expert at a young age. Zach had dark hair with sparkly eyes, and was the unofficial talisman of the Third Platoon.

Mac walked through the untidy living room back into the large kitchen where he found Fletcher and Fry trying to console two female family members. The two DTs gave Mac a nod as they continued to try to take control of the interviews and calm down the relatives of the victim in the front yard.

After several minutes of status quo, Liam said, "Mac, we got this. If you want to check with Barlow to see what else needs to be done."

Mac simply shrugged and retraced his steps to the front porch.

"Hey Sarge, Fletcher, and Fry state they are all set. What else do you need?"

Barlow was talking to Lou, the new DT in the squad.

Lou was very young, and looked young. He resembled an accountant. Approximately 5' 9" tall, average weight with a brown brush cut, and wearing black framed glasses over his light brown colored eyes.

"Oh, good. Take FNG and start doing a neighborhood canvass. Begin with those looky-loos on the tape. For Christ's sake, this happened in broad daylight. There must be a dozen witnesses that saw this thing go down," Barlow said, looking over the top of Lou's prickly head.

"You got it, Sarge," Mac looked at Lou and gestured with his chin down the stairs and back towards the crime scene tape.

Lou followed Mac down the steps. Before they got to the crowd standing behind the tape Lou said: "Why'd he call me FNG?"

"Fucking New Guy," Mac answered, without turning around, surveying the line.

"Sarge doesn't like me?"

"That's not it. It's just you're the new guy. Don't sweat it. Follow me. I have a hunch."

Mac had been looking at some teenage boys standing right in front of the tape line. While Lou was speaking, Mac kept his gaze on them as they noticed him watching them. The kids then nonchalantly moved off the line and started walking down the sidewalk away from the crime scene.

With Lou in tow, Mac again stooped under the plastic yellow tape and quickly walked after the three juveniles.

"Hey, fellas! Wait up!" Mac said, trying to close the gap on the teenagers.

The three boys turned around and waited for Mac and Lou to catch up.

"Thanks! Did you guys see what happened?" Mac asked.

The three boys just looked at each other.

It was a knowing look, and it gave Mac his answer.

"It's okay. You're not in trouble. We're just trying to figure out what happened," Mac followed up.

Now the kids looked back at the crowd to see who was watching this interaction with the two detectives.

"Look, we're not snitches," one of the boys nervously answered.

"Yeah! Snitches get stitches!" another one of the boys interjected.

The three juveniles were around thirteen years old and even though they weren't forthcoming; they were respectful in their demeanor towards the cops.

The kids started walking again towards Cherry Street. Mac followed the teenagers, and Lou followed Mac.

When the entourage got to the house on the southeast corner of East Fayette Street and Cherry Street, the kids climbed halfway up the cement steps from the sidewalk and sat down. It was just steps away from the dark red two-family that occupied this part of the block.

An African-American female poked her head out of the front door of the first-floor entrance and asked, "You alright?"

The kids looked up and the juvenile closest to the house answered, "Yes, Mamma."

Mac walked the rest of the way up the cement stairway. "Hi, ma'am. I'm Detective MacKenna with the Syracuse Police Department. There's been an incident up the street and I was asking the kids if they may have seen anything."

"Well, Charles. Did you tell them what you saw?"

"No, Mamma," Charles said sheepishly.

"You tell them what you told me," The mother said sternly.

"Yes, Mamma."

"Yo, C-Dawg. You got punked by your own mother!" one of the boys whispered more than said.

"Antwan, do I have to call your mother?"

"No, ma'am."

"Alright then. Charles, tell the police what you saw."

“Yes, ma’am.”

Charles went on to say that he was playing on the rock wall across the street waiting for his friends when he heard what sounded like a firecracker go off. He stated when he turned toward the sound he saw a black male in his mid-twenties, 5’ 11” tall, skinny but with a muscular build, having a brush cut with wavy hair, and that he was wearing a white T-shirt and black jeans.

He further stated that this person was holding a rifle against another black male who was standing on the first step of the porch at 1616 East Fayette Street. He said that this male had a brush cut also, and was light-skinned, wearing a De Julio’s T-shirt and blue jeans.

Charles spoke as he looked over from across the street. The man with the De Julio’s T-shirt fell backward into the front yard. He stated that the other man then started kicking the downed man in the face and screaming at him.

He finished up by stating that he ran home, told his mother, and called the 911 Center. Charles specified he did not give the 911 operator his name because he was scared.

Mac had Lou pull his detective ride down around the corner on Cherry Street so Lou could take a written statement on what Charles saw and did. It was done kind of secretly so that everyone at the crime scene didn't see Charles talking to the police in the cop car.

Charles and his mother were really decent people living in a depressed part of the city. It was a less-than-ideal place to live, but they did the right thing and told Mac and Lou what they needed to know. Not everyone in the neighborhood would agree that this was the right thing, though.

Most of the time, the men and women in Major Crimes helped witnesses walk this fine line.

If good people didn't try to take control of their living environment, the bad guys would surely sense this and take over. Crime and the killings would get worse. Without the citizenry cooperating with the cops; the criminal justice system didn't stand a chance.

A suspect was developed by talking to the victim's sisters, along with Charles' description of the suspect. A six-pack photo array was put together and Charles and his mother, yet again, did the right thing and came down to Major Crimes at Police Headquarters.

Charles was shown the photo array and asked if he recognized anyone. He viewed a photographic array on a piece of copy paper with six similar photographs. Mac advised Charles that the person he saw at the homicide may or may not be in there.

He pointed to photograph #1 in the upper lefthand corner of the sheet. When Mac asked him to sign his name over the face of the person he identified; he signed his name and continued to write "Only 80% sure. Not positive. 80%."

This appeared to be at the direction of his mother and agreed upon before they arrived in CID. Mac asked Charles about this extra information he added after the signature.

He stated the incident transpired very fast, that a lot was happening, and that he was scared at the time. Charles again stated that the man in the photograph looked like the man who had the rifle last night and was kicking the other man as he was on the ground.

Again, even though they may have had some

reservations about getting involved, Charles and his mother gave the best assessment they could.

As it turned out, after everyone in Major Crimes got done with their interviews, the suspect thought the victim was having sexual relations with the suspect's girlfriend.

Unfortunately, it was an old story that the cops heard all the time. Countless stabbings, shootings, and deaths were over actual or perceived dalliances that resulted in one or more people in the ground, and others behind bars.

In the end. It was just another statistic in the homicide column at the City of Syracuse Police Department.

Lou was learning as fast as he could, but he definitely should've had more time as a road patrol cop before coming to CID. Yet again, just another part of the never-ending generational cycle that made Major Crimes DTs continue to schlep on with solving the worst of the worst wrongdoings in the city.

The years teach much which the days never know.

- Ralph Waldo Emerson

CHAPTER
FOUR

The day before Halloween, Guinness, the dog, wasn't feeling well. He wasn't eating and had suddenly become lethargic with his stomach feeling rigid. Mac dutifully called the veterinarian and was told to bring him in straight away.

The vet's office was less than two miles down the street in the Village of Camillus. After a quick checkup, the doctor advised that she would like to keep him overnight for observation.

Mac was apprehensive, since Guinness the dog had

never stayed away from home before. But Guinness's sad watery eyes told the story that something was just not right. So, Mac reluctantly agreed. Giving Guinness the dog a scratch behind his ears and a kiss on the snout, telling him he would be back to get him first thing in the morning.

The next day, Mac woke up and called the vet's office as soon as it opened. He wasn't used to not having his faithful companion with him.

"I'm sorry Mr. MacKenna. Guinness passed away last night," the receptionist advised.

"Oh, okay. Can I come get him?" Mac answered in a daze.

"Yes, of course. There is also an outstanding bill for three hundred and eighteen dollars for the tests we ran."

"Um, okay. I'll be right there."

Mac's little voice added, "Talk about insult to injury."

He didn't have time to debate his inner voice. This was devastating news.

Without thinking, Mac got into his car and made

the short two-minute ride to the veterinarian's office. By the time he got there, tears were streaming uncontrollably down his cheeks.

He was only slightly embarrassed to be seen by the medical staff and the waiting pet owners in the waiting room. Mac pulled out his credit card to settle his outstanding charge before picking up the black plastic bag containing his beloved pet and carrying it to his car.

The collar for Guinness, the dog, was resting on top of the bag.

The one-hundred-and-twenty-five-pound death-shrouded package did not seem that heavy. Once more, with tears making it hard to see, Mac commenced the short drive back home with his friend.

The overcast gray and threatening sky seemed à propos; as Mac gently laid Guinness down in the corner of the white picket fence, where he used to lie for hours at a time. He retrieved a spade from the garage and dug a shallow grave; softly placing Guinness within the black bag in the cold ground, before shoveling the dirt back into its place.

Mac, holding the dog collar, kneeled on both knees and said goodbye as the rain started falling from the dark and stormy skies above.

He got up off the ground, wiping his tears and brushing off his knees, thinking about how he was going to do the toughest job of all: tell his children.

*

So, yeah, that was tough. Seeing he had no reason to stay home now, Mac decided he would take a trip to Key West, Florida. It was well overdue.

He had been a cop now for seventeen years and had non-stop raised his children, mostly by himself. Having just turned forty, Mac was alone for the first time since he had married his high school sweetheart when he was eighteen years old.

The freedom felt uncomfortable.

Mac, of course, asked NMI if she wanted to go with him on vacation, but she refused.

Her thirty-fifth birthday had been in July and Mac had made a big deal of it. Taking her out to an exclusive dinner and gifting her with a white gold, diamond, and emerald necklace. It was one of the most expensive presents he had ever given her, having given her plenty. Numerous Gucci watches, Coach purses, as well as other high-end jewelry and clothes over the years, but this was indeed special.

The couple were still married but had been apart for over nine years now. With all the children out of the house; Mac was hoping for a renaissance of their relationship, but something else was going on. He couldn't put his finger on it, but it was certainly there. Mac asked NMI if something else was bothering her, but always got nothing back in return.

Alas, without Guinness the dog, his children, or a love interest, Mac was heading south for a much-needed ten-day vacation.

He had ALWAYS gone on vacation with his children and/or NMI. This would be his first vacation without them; making him feel extremely guilty.

But, after four years of working stabbings, shootings,

robberies, and death scenes; he needed to get away.

As a young cop, he frequently stood in three feet of snow and cold, dreaming about living in Hawaii or Florida, where it was perpetually summer.

He quickly ruled out Hawaii, as it would be forever and a day for his family to come visit from New York State. Florida, it was then.

His paternal grandparents had first rented a house by the beach in Pass-a-Grill, Florida when he was about eleven years old. He, his brother, and two sisters had ridden in a County Squire station wagon all the way from Syracuse in January. Leaving the cold and ice behind and winding up in paradise.

Mac couldn't believe that everyone in the United States wouldn't rather live in this temperate setting. That memory stuck with him.

Later on, his grandparents bought a place to snowbird in Pinellas Park, Florida. Still, in the Tampa Bay region.

He would drive their car down for them so they could fly down. The area always stayed in his head.

Maybe, just maybe, one day.

For now, though, he was going as far south as one could get in the continental United States. The playground of Hemingway, Capote, Frost, Buffett, Chesney, and every other misfit who was lucky enough to get there.

*

Leaving Key West International Airport in the back of his yellow cab in the early afternoon, Mac breathed in the salty air and was relieved to see the shiny ball of light in the cloudless sky. It seemed Central New York was constantly overcast, and the sun was rarely seen.

The cabbie was fittingly playing *A Pirate Looks at Forty* by Jimmy Buffett. Mac wondered if the driver was really into Buffett, or did he do it to increase his tips with the tourists who came to live the lifestyle?

He had booked a condo at the Truman Annex located at the island's western end: once home to the naval base and submarine station the US Navy used during World War II. Truman Annex was established in 1947 as a naval base and submarine station. The base was named after President Harry S. Truman.

Incidentally, Key West was first discovered by Ponce de Leon in 1513. For years, the rights to the Keys went back and forth between Spain and England, until all of Florida was relinquished to the United States in 1819.

Eventually, an American businessman named John Simonton purchased the island of Key West. He understood the possibilities of its deep-water dockage, dividing it into four parts, keeping one for himself and selling the other three to businessmen Fleming, Whitehead, and Green. These four men live on as their surnames are used as Key West thoroughfares.

Mac had rented a spacious room on the second floor of the complex. There was a nice pool centered in the courtyard. Because it was after Labor Day, and therefore considered out of season, the property was affordable and quiet.

For the next ten days, Mac's routine was pretty much the same. He would get up around ten o'clock and go for a three-mile run around the island. His route took him down Southard Street to Whitehead Street, where he would run by The Hemmingway Home and Museum. Then continuing east until he came to The Southernmost Point of the Continental USA marker; whirling left and turning north up South Street, before jogging over some blocks by the coast until he was running by Higgs Beach, before looping back.

His afternoons were spent by the pool reading or going the short distance over to discover the Fort Zachary Taylor Beach area. His condo had a full kitchen, and he stocked up to have breakfast and lunch there.

Mac would then scope out restaurants on Duval Street for late-night dinners before exploring even more bars in the area for adult beverages.

Yes, it was kind of lonely. But the solace was comforting. He didn't have a care in the world and was semi-content to be a solo explorer.

His inner voice, of course, had to interject from time to time. "You're such a loser for being here by yourself!"

But since he didn't rent a car and walked everywhere; he was able to eventually drown it out.

Mac never attempted to pick women up at bars. He felt it to be too cliché. Besides the fact that he was still pining for NMI, he had three sisters and two daughters; and wouldn't want men hitting on them if they decided to go out for a drink.

Not that there was anything wrong with it, he supposed. Men, after all, did it all the time. However, when Mac saw them do it, it didn't seem very genuine at all. It was just a numbers game. The more women they pitched, the greater the odds of someone giving in.

Being Irish Catholic, Mac had unique thoughts of having carnal knowledge with women. The act itself felt like an entwining of souls. He thought that shouldn't be taken lightly.

His inner voice vehemently disagreed.

So, near the end of his trip, he was at his customary spot for his last drink of the evening. The Green Parrot.

The Green Parrot Bar is mythological in the quaint Key West neighborhood. First operated in 1890 as a grocery store, it became The Brown Derby Bar, which submarine sailors frequented after World War Two. In the 1970s, it was renamed the Green Parrot after it became a hotspot for hippies, bikers, and free spirits.

The Parrot was not on Duval Street like all the other fabled places that tourists flock to, but on Whitehead Street, just a block from the Truman Annex. Its close proximity to Mac's lodging made it a logical place to stop on the way back to his room.

The short framed white washed boarded structure - with Kelly green accent paint - opened up to a large circular bar and a stage set off to the side for performers. The hefty, boarded windows were perpetually raised on hooks, so the inside felt like the outside. The front and side doors were always open during business hours.

The bartenders were all middle-aged white guys who had been there forever and seen it all. The bar stayed open until 4 AM and also was a popular spot for other hospitality workers when they got done with their shifts.

Since this was part of his routine, the bartenders knew his drink order and a little of his backstory. They were very welcoming and Mac was content to just people watch until his little voice told him it was time to go home.

On this particular night, Mac had done some lengthy exploring of Irish Kevin's', Sloppy Joe's, and the Hogg's Breath Saloon. He had just finished a conversation with one of the bartenders about how their night had gone, when they walked in.

The bar wasn't that busy for a late Tuesday night. Mac was nursing his Captain Morgan and Diet Coke in a pint glass at the end of the circular bar.

It was 2:45 AM and the bartender that had just served Mac finished wiping down the bar and walked nonplussed back to the new customers.

Mac obviously knew the history of Key West. Chiefly, that alternative lifestyles were celebrated here openly. But it being the off-season and all, there hadn't been anything that outrageous during his stay to mention. Until now.

The five men could have been the current defensive line for the Buffalo Bills football team. The four white guys and the sole African-American male were all over six foot four, weighing in at a healthy three hundred pounds. Their stature was raised even higher because they were all wearing different varieties of two-inch, size fourteen woman's heels.

They were in complete drag with the accompaniment of thick make-up, wigs, and dresses.

Mac wasn't sure if it was a gag, they lost a bet, OR they were the real deal. So, the prudent thing to do was not to stare and to find something else to look at. Fast!

The bartender acted like this happens all the time—which it most unquestionably does in Key West—and served them their drinks. Surprisingly, they all ordered bottled Bud Lights.

Shifting in his seat to watch the pool game behind him, Mac caught movement out of the corner of his eye. Before he could finish the sip on his drink; the African American male had sashayed down the bar and was looming over Mac.

"Can I buy you a drink?" Came the rich baritone voice from above.

Now Mac didn't want to look over, but he really didn't have a choice.

The drag queen was standing only inches apart, waiting on an answer.

Mac smiled, trying to bide some time. Should he offend the Bill Willis look-a-like or should he just pretend that he doesn't understand the question?

Wait, Mac's little voice was getting ready to add some advice. "You're on your own, pal. The guy can destroy us all on his own. He doesn't even need the other lineman to do it. I'm not getting blamed for this one!"

"Thanks a lot," Mac mumbled, before realizing that he was talking out loud to the behemoth and not his annoying and less-than-helpful inner voice.

Before the imagined NFL player could engage any further, the merciful bartender came back down the bar. "Hey Bud! That guy's not into it."

"Pity," came the response, before the black drag queen rejoined his friends at the other end of the bar.

Not knowing whether to be flattered or terrified, Mac finished up his drink, tipping out the bartender twenty dollars for his aid, and leaving for the safety of the street-lit landscape. As he walked back to his condo Mac decided that Key West was amusing, as in it's a remarkable place to visit–but I wouldn't want to live here, kind of way.

Never go on trips with anyone you do not love.

- Ernest Hemingway

CHAPTER
FIVE

When Mac got home from his Key West trip, it was back to work and an empty house. There was no word on any movement on the Sergeant's List, or the other promotional exams; although city hall gave permission for another police academy class. Thus, Major Crimes detectives were assigned background investigations on prospective new hires for the department.

These assignments were done when time permitted between the criminal investigations they already had.

The department allocated overtime for the background checks, which made the task a little bit more palatable.

When one takes the test to be a police officer in New York State, they open up their personal life to inordinate scrutiny. It is not for the timid.

And, even some are arrested in the process...

Thousands of potential police candidates would sign up with the Onondaga County Personnel Department to take the police officer civil service exam, which was given twice a year.

Applicants had to be United States citizens, between twenty and thirty-five years old, who lived within Onondaga County or one of his contiguous counties. They would also have to possess a valid New York State Driver's license.

Those lucky enough to pass the written exam would be invited to take the Physical Fitness Test, also given by Onondaga County. Which consisted of sit-ups, push-ups, and a 1.5-mile run. All were timed events, and each candidate had to record a minimum number or time for their age category.

Of those who passed both assessments; they would be invited to an informational meeting at the City of Syracuse Police Department to outline which procedures would come next in the hiring progression.

Successful applicants could not be convicted felons or even have arrest records for serious misdemeanors. However, even an arrest without a conviction usually meant that they weren't getting invited to take part in the rest of the hiring procedures.

Usually, this whittled down the list to a few hundred. Then would come the Psychological Evaluation, Medical Standards, and finally, the Background Investigation.

This would bring the number of potential cops down to about one hundred candidates. Not everyone would get backgrounded. Those scoring in the 90% - 100% would get processed first by investigators. If there weren't enough entrants, it would go to 80% - 90%. It rarely, if ever, got to the 70% - 80% percentile.

If the contender made it through the background investigation unscathed, they would have to take a Polygraph Test. This is what usually got some applicants expelled and arrested.

The polygraphers were seasoned detectives who were very good at their jobs. The test was a minuscule part of the exam. The real art came into the interview leading up to the test itself: reading people and seeing what made them uncomfortable was what the examiners would key on. The polygraphers could almost sense that something was off when it came to certain subject matter.

The subjects broached in the interview would consist of honesty, narcotics, abhorrent behavior, and sex.

It seemed what tripped up the contestants that made it this far was overwhelmingly: SEX.

One twenty-year-old male candidate admitted to having sexual relations with a sixteen-year-old girl. The age of consent in New York State is seventeen.

Another male applicant admitted to burglarizing his next-door neighbor's house to steal female undergarments so that he could masturbate to them. That would be Burglary in the Second Degree.

Yet, another male candidate took it up a notch by admitting to bestiality with Fido, the family dog, whereas another went for having sex with his girlfriend's cat. Both, equally, against the law in New York State.

The detectives who had done the successful background checks to get them to the polygraph were unmercifully tortured by their fellow DTs in the bullpen. Little could they have known about these obscure sexual deviant behaviors; but cops being cops, they were reminded of their transgression for years to come.

With this in mind, Mac was traveling on his rest day down Route 81 South on his way to Dundee, New York, to conclude his background investigation on police candidate Timothy Norris.

What follows is a typical background investigation report on a prospective employee for the City of Syracuse Police Department:

A CHAIRS (Criminal History Arrest Incident Reporting System) and Person Name Search in the Onondaga County area for the past ten years showed negative for any contact with law enforcement agencies.

A check with the New York State Police Investigator Randy Newman (Bureau of Criminal Investigation) (607) 243-1772 - in the Dundee, New York area showed negative contact.

A check with the Yates County Sheriff's Department Lieutenant Pitcher (315) 536-5142, showed that Mr. Norris' only contact with their department was for a minor vehicle accident and a vehicle lockout. There was no criminal contact with their agency.

A Department of Motor Vehicles check showed that Mr. Norris possesses a valid New York State Class D License with no traffic infractions.

On 01DEC02, I conducted a Residency Verification/History and Summary check by traveling to Mr. Norris' residence located at 810 Beam Rd. Dundee, New York. No one was at home during my visit.

On 01DEC02, I also conducted a Neighborhood Canvass of Mr. Norris' neighborhood to confirm his residency and character.

Sara Donovan 101 Bigelow Ave. Dundee, NY 14837 (607) 243-5213 - Spoke with Ms. Donovan as she was working as a clerk at the Cluster Pines Store located at 5430 Route 14 Dundee, NY 14837. Ms. Donovan stated that the Norris family was well-liked in the community and that Mr. Norris was a very nice man.

Dale Guerra 733 E. Lake Rd. Penn Yan, NY 14527 (607) 243-7900 - Spoke with Mr. Guerra who was a customer in the Cluster Pines Store. He stated that the family was nice and that he believed that one of Mr. Norris's sisters was already a police officer in Oswego County.

Gregory Mora 918 Beam Rd. Dundee, NY 14837 (607) NO PHONE—Spoke with Mr. Norris' next-door neighbor, who stated that he had lived there for approximately one month. He stated he knew Mr. Norris from High School and that Mr. Norris' name was Timothy Norris then. Mr. Mora stated that Mr. Norris did not cause any trouble in High School and that since he had lived next door to him, there have been no problems at the Norris residence.

Zakaria Tate Residence 6692 Lakemont-Himrod Road Dundee, NY 14837 (607) 243-8448—Spoke with Mr. Tate via phone after leaving a business card in his door to call me regarding Mr. Norris' possible employment with the Syracuse Police Department. Mr. Tate stated that Mr. Norris would make a great candidate for the police department. He further stated that Mr. Norris and his family have lived next to him for approximately 5-7 years and that they are great neighbors.

Mrs. Tanya Berg 5111 Himrod Road Dundee, NY 14837 (607) 243-0981—Returned a phone call to Sgt. Merrill (CID) regarding one of my business cards left in her door. She stated that Mr. Norris is a "Great Kid".

On 05DEC02 at 0945 hours, a check with Investigator Sgt. Rhys Cox (TRAINING) showed that he did not have any concerns with Mr. Norris at this point.

On 05DEC02 at 1549 hours, I spoke with Mr. Norris via phone regarding his possible employment with the Syracuse Police Department. Mr. Norris expressed concern with the pending polygraph examination. He stated that while in High School when he was eighteen (18) years old, he was dating a fourteen (14) year old girlfriend. Mr. Norris stated he had a sexual relationship with this girl, who he identified as Rose

Zhang. Mr. Norris stated that this relationship was consensual, but that he knew it was wrong because of the age difference. Mr. Norris stated he was to meet with Sgt. Barlow on 06DEC02 and said that he would relay the information he had told me regarding his apprehension with the polygraph test. Mr. Norris stated that if he was offered the job with the city, he would move his family to Onondaga County to accommodate his employment.

The preceding synopsis is a compilation of the duties assigned to me regarding Mr. Norris as a possible police candidate with the City of Syracuse Police Department.

Although Mac thought the investigation was going in Mr. Norris' favor, that last phone conversation was the death knell of his law enforcement career. It was commendable that he acknowledged it prior to his polygraph examination—which, incidentally, kept him from being arrested by the Syracuse Police Department—but Rape in the Second Degree had an open-ended statute of limitation on it.

The SPD Training Division devotedly reported the

criminal act to the Yates County Sheriff's Department for follow-up. Without cooperation from Mr. Norris and the alleged victim, the case wasn't going anywhere toward a prosecution. But, yet again, it was a cautionary tale about how one indiscretion from years ago could derail a criminal justice career.

The public was blissfully unaware of the scrutiny given to potential police officer candidates. Great strides were taken to assure the community that the cop in uniform they saw in the marked car, or the detective in the suit with the notepad, was vetted to the nth degree.

Even so, the police department is a microcosm of society as a whole. Some unsuitable personalities still make it through the small cracks in the formidable system of checks and balances.

Of those, some would be bounced out of the police academy when those flaws were exposed. Others wouldn't make it through the Field Training Officer Program once they graduated from the academy.

Yet others would be reported by their fellow cop brethren after they were On the Job if repugnant behavior was discovered down the line in their career.

To the background investigating detectives; upholding the public trust was a privilege, and it all started and ended with the pride of those rank-and-file officers that guarded that sacred trust to wear a revered police badge.

Love all, trust a few, do wrong to none.

-William Shakespeare

CHAPTER SIX

Coleman's Pub was the epicenter of Tipperary Hill in the City of Syracuse. Irish immigrants mostly from County Tipperary, Ireland, originally settled the far westside city neighborhood. A large number of those migrants had worked on the Erie Canal in the early 1800s.

Mac's great-grandfather, whom he was named after, had immigrated to the states from County Limerick, Ireland, in 1903, when he was twenty-two years old. He was a farmer on his parent's land in the old country and was a laborer in his newly adopted home.

To this day, Tipp Hill, as it is commonly known, is still home to many of Irish lineage. The area is plentiful of Gaelic bars and restaurants, but Coleman's was Mac's local, as it held a special place in his heart.

His name's sake had drunk here at the end of prohibition in 1933. The place had changed dramatically since then, but he felt a familiar connection to the establishment that his grandfather and his father had likewise patronized.

It was New Year's Eve and Mac had been able to finagle a night off from Major Crimes to meet his good mates from SPD at Coleman's to ring in the new year. Of course, he would've much rather spent the holiday with NMI, but she apparently had other plans.

Mac braved the northerly snow-enhanced wind as he made his way from the side parking lot, where he parked his black Porsche, to the heavy wooden stained glass front door of the tavern. He briefly shook hands with Frankie the bouncer, before stomping off the snow from his dress shoes and continuing into the raucous warm bar area to search for his friends.

The smell of food from the kitchen mixed with the cigarette smoke from the pub as Mac made his way through the disorderly crowd. The *Mere Mortals* played in the far corner, competing to be heard over the excited revelers. Craic was everywhere within the Irish establishment.

Mac found Kylen "Hammer" Duffy, Scott Sutton, Tatum Fuller, Katy Hill, Roderick Dalton, Gil Lockhart, and his old partner Francis Tucker, standing by the waitress station at the bar, situated by the back, sunken dining room. The rich mahogany bar top held most of their drinks and those of their dates.

Hammer had just recently married his long-time girlfriend, and Hammer's old partner, Scott Sutton, had done the same. Mac's old sex crimes partner, Katy, was with his good friend, Tatum Fuller. Gil Lockhart had been married before he transferred up from downstate.

Francis had his steady girl with him; and Dalton, a confirmed lifetime bachelor, always had a new girl on his arm.

Mac, as usual, was stag.

The cops and their dates wore clothing that matched that of the other customers in the establishment this evening.

The men wore suits, with dress shirts, ties, and dress shoes. The women wore form-fitting glittery dresses and heels. Of course, the women had their hair and nails done to perfection. The guys were content to have visited the barber.

The *Mere Mortals* were doing a cover of *Complicated* by Avril Lavigne, as Mac shook hands and gave hugs out on the way to the bar.

He caught AJ the bartender's eye and received an acknowledgment from him. Less than a minute later, a Captain Morgan and Diet Coke in a pint glass with a lime wedge on the rim was in front of him. Since the ticket price included drinks for the evening, he gave AJ a twenty for the tip jar.

"Where's NMI?" Hammer asked as he left his wife with one of the other girls.

"She didn't say," Mac said, as he took a sip and looked over the crowd.

"Dude, you got to quit that!"

"Yeah, I know. But it's complicated..."

"What's complicated?" Francis asked, walking into the conversation to get another Bud Light from AJ.

"He's alone again," Hammer said. "He's got to move on from NMI and find another relationship. The one he has with her is toxic."

Taking the beer bottle from AJ, "You know, Kylen does have a point. It's been what? Ten years? What's the end game?" Francis said, taking his own sip from the amber bottle.

"Guys, it's just..."

"We know. Complicated!" They both said at once.

"Hey, who's Gil with back there in the corner?" Mac said, hoping to change the subject.

"That's Melissa, the Channel 9 NEWS reporter," Hammer answered with a sly grin.

"His wife didn't make it?" Mac followed up, somewhat perplexed.

"Dude, since he's been the PIO for the department,

he's been stepping out with anything in a skirt," Dalton answered.

"Yeah, he's apparently taking advantage of his local celebrity. He's on the television more than the chief, so everyone thinks HE'S the chief," Tatum said, as he squeezed Katy Hill a little closer.

Mac gave Katy an - *are you kidding me?* look.

"I know nothing," Katy said, somewhat irritated with the direction the conversation was going.

The cops at the bar all got caught by Gil staring at him and his paramour. He seemed unfazed by the attention, smiling back at them like the cat that ate the canary, raising a glass in their direction.

*

Mac wasn't only an odd man out because he was dateless; all his good friends had also been recently made sergeants. He was still sitting third on a terminal promotional list that wasn't going anywhere.

"What's going on with your kids?" Dalton asked, joining the growing conversation.

"Bridget is still in Florida, living with my sister. I guess things are going okay. She doesn't really check in with me.

Joseph is at Utica College at Syracuse University. He gave up on the lacrosse team because he didn't like the coach. Instead, he joined the golf team. His grades aren't the best, but he's still hanging in there.

Elizabeth is still living at her mother's house. She doesn't reach out at all either."

"Sorry Mac," Dalton said, shuffling his feet on his long lanky body.

"No worries. Things change. Kids grow up. That's supposed to happen, I guess. How's being a boss in the K-9 unit?"

Dalton had been a K-9 handler for five years before being promoted. He was lucky enough to keep his dog and remain in the unit after the promotion.

"Nothing really has changed. I help Timmy with scheduling and training, but everything remains the same. I love it!"

"Good for you Rod. I'm jealous," Mac said, as he playfully clapped him on the shoulder.

Mac kept his back against the bar, in the middle of his circle of friends, as they rotated in and out, away from their significant others. The band played on into the night as the ballet of assorted Coleman's regulars continually moved around them.

A couple of girls caught Mac's eye from time to time, but all he could do was sheepishly smile and look away. He was hopeful that NMI would stop by the house at the end of the night, but that was more than likely a losing proposition.

"Hey, what's going on with the Navy?" Francis asked, getting drinks for him and his girl this time.

Mac had enlisted with the United States Naval Reserve after getting cold-called by a recruiter four years earlier. He was thirty-six at the time, with no previous military service. Mac was lucky enough to become an Intelligence Specialist First Class in four years, coming off active duty after 9/11 last summer.

"You know, since I worked for NCIS on active duty, I've been trying to find angles to switch over to them in the reserves from the Defense Intelligence Agency. My Intel officers and chiefs have been supportive, but they have been vocal about trying to keep me in the unit."

"Hey, that's great! Any idea how long that would take?"

Francis was an officer with the Army Reserves and was a Gulf War veteran.

"Not really. As of now, there are no open billets in the northeast. I'm going to have to make a move sooner rather than later, though. To be an NCIS special agent, I would have to attend the Federal Law Enforcement Training Center in GLYNCO, Georgia. The FLETC academy is just short of six months long, and I'm not getting any younger."

"No sweat Patrick, you're in great shape. You shouldn't have any problems with another academy," Francis said, smiling, getting his drinks from AJ and moving back towards his date.

But Mac was worried. He never thought he would get

a crack at being a special agent. His military career had just sort of fallen into his lap late in life. He was so close, but time was certainly not his friend.

Just before midnight, the band was playing a rendition of *She Hates Me* by *Puddle of Mudd*, when Mac snuck out the back-alley door. The last place he wanted to be was in the middle of a bar full of people where everyone was kissing their significant others, and he was standing awkwardly alone in the middle of it.

This had been his practice for the last decade. Standing alone in a darkened alley having a cigarette while he texted his children wishing them a Happy New Year!

Even though he certainly wasn't a smoker, he would have a cigarette from time to time when he was drinking. Marlboro Ultra Lights were the lightest cigarettes he could find and were his poison of choice.

So, at the stroke of twelve, he held a cigarette in one hand while looking up at the crisp, cool starry sky and the glowing crescent moon. He held a silver 1939 Liberty dollar in the other hand. His mother, Serlait, had given him the coin years earlier. It was an old wife's tale that if one held a silver coin on New Year's Eve at midnight, it would bring prosperity in the coming year.

Mac wasn't sure it worked, but he hadn't been completely broke since she gave it to him. Always looking on the upside, Mac held the coin firmly as he extinguished the cig under his foot and began the diligent texting of his children in the promise of a clean slate and a prosperous new year.

Few of us can stand prosperity. Another man's, I mean.

- Mark Twain

CHAPTER SEVEN

The last Sunday in January is customarily reserved for the National Football League's championship game. This year, the big game was played in San Diego, California, and featured the Oakland Raiders against the Tampa Bay Buccaneers. Even though the Raiders were favored by four points, the Bucs crushed them 48 - 21 to win Super Bowl XXXVII.

But that's not why the men and women of Major Crimes remembered about it. It was the day of one of the most gruesome crimes committed in the City of

Syracuse. Mac was thankful it wasn't his case, but even for the bit player DTs, it was hard to take.

That Monday morning, it was all hands-on deck for the Criminal Investigations Division. Mac, like most of his cop sisters and brethren, was called in from their Rest Days, or prior to the start of their upcoming shift in the CID.

The victim's mother had been eagerly anticipating her daughter's arrival at her home for a lively Super Bowl party that Sunday. She thought it extremely odd when her daughter didn't show up, but became panicked when she learned she hadn't arrived for work early Monday morning.

Her mother lived a very short distance away from her daughter's residence. Unfortunately, upon making the quick trip over to check on her, she found her gruesomely murdered daughter's body inside the apartment. The explicit way in which the victim had been killed was extremely troubling to the experienced Major Crimes detectives.

Like most cases, the victim's mother called the 911 Center upon discovering her only child. The 911 dispatcher for Channel #3 sent two marked patrol units to 600 James Street Apartment #613 for a Check the Status Call / Possible DOA.

The day road patrol sergeant didn't need his units to call him to that location, as he was already in route. Upon his arrival, the uniformed supervisor immediately called the 'House Mouse' in Major Crimes and advised that this wasn't your ordinary homicide scene.

Captain Walsh would normally only go to a death investigation scene if his detective sergeants requested him to be there. The captain, after hearing what the veteran uniformed sergeant had stated to the 'House Mouse'; was en route from Headquarters within seconds.

The road patrol cops didn't have to check the body for a pulse. It was overtly obvious that the soul had left the abused shell of the woman's body long ago. They did a very cursory check of the small apartment, looking for other victims or possibly the suspect, before backing out and securing the scene for the arrival of the detectives.

They didn't have to wait long for the cadre of plain clothes DTs arrival on the scene.

The seven-story red brick apartment complex on the southeast corner of James Street and North McBride Street looked stately, but had outlived its original appearance decades ago. Even though James Street was a major thoroughfare in a business district that traversed down the northside of the city; very few people would voluntarily stop in the neighborhood after dark.

Those that did would overwhelmingly search for prostitutes that hung in the shadows.

The unfortunate DT that caught the case was Detective Wendel Garner from CID Second Platoon. Mac had worked closely with Garner on the Third Platoon, and he knew all too well about the good-natured German with the brush mustache. Garner took great pride in his heritage.

It took Mac about fifteen minutes to get into his sports coat, dress shirt, tie, slacks, and dress shoes; before showing up at the soon-to-be notorious crime scene.

Mac skated his way, more than walked, down the icy front sidewalk to The James apartment building. He found Garner under the black canvass awning labeled

600, standing off to the side of the bosses who were deep in conversation.

Mac, wearing his signature black bowler hat with a red feather in the band, pulled his Hickey Freeman coat a little tighter as he avoided the supervisors and addressed Detective Wendel Garner.

"Herr Wendel, did you catch this?"

"Oh, shit Mac, yeah!" Garner said in a hushed voice, nudging him a little further from the huddling bosses.

It was so cold that Mac could see mist coming from Wendel's mouth as he spoke. "This is Bad. Real bad. Like deranged shit bad."

Mac blew on his hands, trying to stay warm. "Like what?"

"Like depraved sex shit. The vic was stabbed multiple times, then posed naked in the middle of the kitchen. There's blood splatter everywhere and pools of blood all over the floor."

"Oh fuck! I'm not going in," Mac said, shaking his head back and forth while stomping his feet to stay warm.

"Nobody's going in this time. We've got it locked down for the Crime Lab. This is going to take a long time to process before we move the body. It's just God awful in there."

"What have you got so far?"

"She was most likely violated and killed sometime Sunday. Her mother found the body and was just taken down to CID by patrol units.

"The worst part, she was eviscerated. That's what probably killed her, but we'll have to wait on the M.E. to verify that," Garner finished up, shaking his frazzled longish brown hair on the thirty-eight-year-old detective, who was visibly older after witnessing the senseless carnage from the apartment high above.

"Hey, Mac! Track down the property manager and find out how the electric key card system works here," Captain Walsh said, before going back to speaking with the detective sergeants.

"On it, Cap," Mac said, giving Garner a nod as he grabbed the ajar front door and entered the building.

Tracking down the property manager who was

standing outside his basement apartment; Mac learned from the manager that an off-site security company managed the electric key card entry system. The manager gave him the info on the security company and victim's key fob number to the doors. Mac called the security company using his CID cell phone and requested all the access sheets for the weekend.

As it turned out, there was an access point at the front door and the rear entrance. The security company, Sonitrol, explained that the computerized chip systems for each access point would only hold the last one thousand entries to each door. By the time Sonitrol captured the data requested by SPD; the front door had exhausted almost everything from the preceding weekend due to the never-ending police activity in the building.

Sonitrol advised that the victims' entries from the front door could not be located and that she had apparently not used the rear entrance to the apartment building. The representative further stated that there were no video cameras at the complex.

And so, the investigation went like that...

For two weeks, the Major Crimes detectives put everything else aside they could and worked the James Street homicide night and day. The case was complicated due to the victims' lifestyle and the volume of potential suspects because of it.

According to everyone the DTs spoke with; the victim was sexually promiscuous and had carnal relations with just about anyone that struck her fancy. Men and women. These could be a onetime chance encounter on the street, to a string of very short-term simultaneous boyfriends or girlfriends that changed weekly.

This was a nightmare scenario for a sexual assault murder investigation.

Although, the victim's loose dating routine obviously played into her tragic and untimely demise; she most certainly didn't deserve to lose her life over it.

The detectives diligently tried to identify everyone connected with her; which were dozens upon dozens. And those were the ones they knew about. There was nothing on social media or on her phone that pointed one way or another. It was just interview everyone and see what didn't track.

They all knew, detectives and supervisors alike, that it was no way to run a fruitful homicide investigation. But it was all they had to work with.

Even though DNA testing was in its infancy, nothing recovered by the Crime Lab was helpful to the murder investigation. After two weeks of nothing, this was a huge disappointment to the DTs working the case.

They were getting nowhere.

But one thing was certain among the men and women detectives in the bullpen of CID. This didn't appear to be the slayer's first kill, and if they didn't identify them, it undoubtedly wouldn't be their last.

All the particulars were eventually plugged into VICAP.

The Violent Criminal Apprehension Program is a component of the United States Federal Bureau of Investigation. The FBI is in charge of the analysis of national serial violent and sexual crimes, based in the Critical Incident Response Group's National Center for the Analysis of Violent Crime in Quantico, Virginia.

VICAP identifies violent patterns or behaviors that may link a suspect to multiple cases in different jurisdictions. Therefore, providing shared information by dispersed law enforcement agencies and increasing the solvability rate for each case.

After several weeks, Mac ran into Wendel Garner in the stairwell of the PSB Headquarters building as they were walking up and down in different directions. They paused on the converging landing between the second and third floors.

"I saw the pictures of the vic and the homicide scene from James Street. I wish I hadn't. Any viable leads?" Mac asked, trying to catch his breath from the walk-up.

"Yeah, I can't get that shit out of my head, either. I'm afraid this is going to end up being a cold case. There's just too many parties of interest and no physical evidence to link anyone to it," Wendel said, adjusting his tie with the hand that wasn't holding the vanilla-colored case file.

"No hits on VICAP?"

"None yet. I would've thought something would

have linked with the way this was carried out.

I'm guessing that they must have been some serial killer looking for a hooker when they came upon her instead. They weren't from the area with no connections to the victim, and they're in the wind," Wendel said, as he continued down the cement stairs to the first floor.

Unbeknownst to Garner, the case would continue to linger, haunting the detectives who had been involved since the beginning for many years to follow.

Mac thought it was unfathomable that a crime of this magnitude would go unresolved in the modern age. Realizing that the general public remained blissfully unaware, he and his fellow DTs understood the true extent of the evil that roamed the world.

If the James Street victim had any inkling of what the detectives knew; she wouldn't have put herself in the position she did on Super Bowl Sunday of 2003. She assuredly would've gone to her mom's for the party instead, avoiding the terminal meeting of the sinister, unknown subject sent to her from hell.

Fear is pain arising from the anticipation of evil.

- Aristotle

CHAPTER EIGHT

As spring sprung in 2003, homicides kept popping up like daisies for the Major Crimes detectives. Cops were always asked, "Why are the prisons so full?" And the cops would dutifully answer, "Because most criminals aren't all that bright." This next case would encapsulate that theory.

Literally, at the beginning of the CID Third Platoon shift; detectives were called to AAA Auto Sales located at 1977 Erie Boulevard East for a homicide investigation. The owner/victim, Pacey Andrews, had been shot at point-blank range five times during a customer dispute with Keyon Moore.

The dispute had been going on for weeks. Keyon Moore had dropped off two Chevrolet Camaro's to be worked on mechanically by Pacey Andrews. As the project progressed, Mr. Andrews advised Mr. Moore that he was not able to successfully cannibalize parts from one of the Camaros to restore the other. The restoration price was going up based on Mr. Andrews locating and buying parts for the venture.

This change in plan had frustrated Mr. Moore. To the point that he approached other mechanics in the city, trying to relocate the restoration project to another business. In his conversations with the other business owners, he had declared, "I'll kill Pacey for screwing me over on those cars!"

Numerous customers of Mr. Andrew's shop had heard the two arguing. In one instance, a customer observed the two physically fighting in the parking lot of the business just two days before the murder.

It was unclear why Mr. Andrews didn't just refuse to do any more work for Moore, nor why he hadn't called the police after the verbal arguments or the physical altercation.

Within forty-five minutes after the DTs arrived on scene, they had identified Keyon Moore as an obvious person of interest in the killing. Since Mr. Moore was a frequent flyer with the Syracuse Police Department, an address was located on the north side of the city for him. In short order, several detectives were directed to try to locate the person of interest.

Detective Sergeant Bruce Merrill had teamed Mac up with Perla "Pocahontas" Hamilton, Tabitha Cherry, and Ian Atkinson. He had known and worked with these detectives on the evening shift for years.

Perla "Pocahontas" Hamilton was a tough, formidable detective who had come from the Special Investigations Division. The 5' 8" tall and solidly built ex-drug cop with hazel eyes and a short brown bob hairstyle, commanded respect. Mac had first met her when he completed a college internship with SPD when he was working for the Town of Camillus Police Department. Perla wasn't fast out of the gate, but she could wield a Streamlight like a lightsaber in a fight. Her nickname had been given to her by the city residents—thinking that she was Native American—which she wasn't; but she embraced the moniker just the same.

Tabitha Cherry was also one of the few women assigned to CID. She confidently stood 5' 7" tall, a muscular build with long blonde hair and blue eyes. Tabitha had been a product of one of the first city police academies when SPD pulled out of the OCSD-run training facility. She was hard-hitting and held her own. It wasn't easy being a female in a male dominated profession, but she made no excuses and looked for no favors. She did the job just like the boys.

Ian Atkinson sported a brush cut on his blonde hair and had been a short-lived partner of Mac's while the department assigned him briefly to the Fourth Platoon on road patrol. Ian had an ever-present grin and was seldom rattled.

The ad hoc team was directed to Mr. Moore's last known address of 400 Griffith Street.

The robin's egg blue single-family home on the raised corner lot looked quiet when the team pulled up. Mac had jumped in with Ian, leaving his CID ride at the crime scene. Tabitha had climbed in with Pocahontas for the short six-minute ride.

Pocahontas and Tabitha parked outside the front entrance, walking up the five-cement white-colored stairs from the sidewalk that brought them to the wooden porch steps of the 1950s-era home.

Mac and Ian had instinctively pivoted off their play and parked around the corner on Craig Street. Quietly walking down another row of square flat stones set in the uncut grass that led around to the side and back of the residence.

Banging could be heard on the aluminum storm door as Mac and Liam covered each corner of the target house; watching the windows for movement while trying to shield themselves from taking any live fire from the home.

After several minutes of unresponsiveness, Pocahontas called on Channel (CID) #5, "No joy. You guys can come back around."

The detectives gathered in the home's front to figure out their next move. All four DTs wearily watched the front of the house while scanning the street for pedestrians and vehicles.

"What now?" Tab addressed the group.

"Do we have any other locations to check?" Ian asked.

"Nope. This is the best one we've got," Pocahontas said, watching the front door.

"How about we drive out and I'll come back on foot through the backyards of Cleveland Avenue I'll set up in the 100 block of Craig Street."

I can cover the front and some of the side of the house. I can call you guys in by radio if I see anyone coming or going," Mac quietly said, looking up and down the street.

"We really don't have anything else. I'll give the Sarge a call and let him know what we're up to," Pocahontas said, with nods all around.

Everyone regained their positions in the CID rides and egressed the area. Ian dropped Mac off two blocks away and he made his way surreptitiously through the side and backyards until Mac was standing on the side of a home in the 100 block of Craig Street. Bushes and a large oak tree gave him some camouflage from curious eyes.

"I'm set," he whispered over his portable police radio.

"Copy," Ian acknowledged.

"Received. We're set up on Butternut Street. Just let us know," Tab said.

They didn't have to wait long.

Twenty minutes later, a newer green Subaru pulled up to the front of the house. A middle-aged white guy got out and went into the home. A minute later, he came back out accompanied by a Native American female about twenty years of age.

"Okay, I've got a green Subaru that pulled up. It's occupied by a middle-aged white male and a young Native American female," Mac said over the portable.

Both units copied Mac's radio transmission and arrived in front of the home before the Subaru could go anywhere.

Mac stayed where he was and observed the

interaction.

The DTs exited their vehicles and walked up on the Subaru as the occupants exited to meet with the cops.

"I'm Mr. Moore's attorney. My name is Clarence Darrow. Can I help you?"

Ian, Pocahontas, and Tab bewilderedly just looked at each other, and then back at the lawyer. Nothing says, "Hey! I did it!" like contacting an attorney directly after you commit a heinous act.

"Yes, we're detectives with the Syracuse Police Department. We've been trying to get in touch with Mr. Moore. Do you know where he is?" Pocahontas asked.

"Yes," came the only response from the lawyer.

"Could you tell us?" Ian prodded.

"I'm afraid not. What is this regarding?"

"It's an ongoing investigation. We'd like to ask Mr. Moore some questions pertaining to our case. Who's this?" Tabitha inquired, nodding to the Native American woman at his side.

"This is Mr. Moore's live-in girlfriend, who resides

with him at this house. I represent both of them, and I'm not permitting you to speak to either of them at this time," Mr. Darrow said, somewhat smugly.

"Counselor, this is a homicide case. Are you obstructing our investigation?" Pocahontas interjected, stepping in a little on Mr. Darrow.

"Not at all. I'm just looking out for my client's rights. Do you have an arrest warrant for Mr. Moore, or a search warrant for the premise?"

"Not at this time. We wanted to get Mr. Moore's side of the story before we leaped to any conclusions." Ian said, trying a more conciliatory tone with the intercessor.

"Well, I'm afraid we're at an impasse. Mr. Moore is currently unavailable at this time."

"Can I go?" The Native American young lady nervously asked Mr. Darrow.

"I can't see why not. You're not under arrest, and I'm not letting you answer any of their questions."

The Native American girl looked from Mr. Darrow to the semi-circle of police detectives, shrugged, and started walking down the street away from the home, using the sidewalk.

This was obviously frustrating for the DTs. Never before had this happened to any of them in their long careers.

Just then, the on-call Death Duty DA, Rory, and the Chief DA for the Homicide Bureau, Steve, from the Onondaga County District Attorney's office pulled up in a county car in front of the suspect's house.

Mac's little voice wondered, "What the heck is going on?"

Tabitha walked away from the group and gave the DAs an update on what had just transpired with Mr. Darrow. The DAs explained they were at the crime scene when they heard over the police radio that there was activity at the suspect's residence and decided to stop by to see if they could be of any assistance.

They called Mr. Darrow over to them, and Tabitha went back to Ian and Pocahontas.

After a brief conversation with Mr. Darrow, Mac could see him pull out his cell phone and walk a little way away from the DA's. Mr. Darrow had a brief conversation on his phone before returning to the DAs.

Mr. Darrow chatted with the DAs for a minute more before getting back into this Subaru and pulling away from the curb. The DAs had a quick chat with Ian, Pocahontas, and Tab before getting back into their own vehicle and leaving the scene as well.

The DTs saddled up back into their CID rides, leaving Mac scratching his chin, trying to make sense of what had just happened.

Before long, Mac's cell phone buzzed in his inside coat pocket.

Ian explained to Mac about Mr. Darrow, Mr. Moore's girlfriend, and the conversations the DAs had with Mr. Darrow.

It was relayed to the cops that at the DA's request, Mr. Darrow called Mr. Moore and attempted to have him surrender himself. This attempt was unsuccessful, but Mr. Moore reportedly agreed to turn himself in tomorrow morning at CID.

Ian said that Detective Sergeant Bruce Merrill had been updated, but still wanted Mac to stay in his surveillance position to try to nab Mr. Moore tonight, if possible. Ian in his car would sit over on Park Street, and Pocahontas and Tabitha would go back over and sit on Butternut Street.

Mac was no stranger to doing surveillances, especially working Anti-Crime and Narcotics. He had even hidden in full police uniform in a tree while trying to apprehend a burglary suspect when he was a Camillus cop.

So, he settled in for the wait.

Sure enough, about two hours later, right after dark, Mr. Moore came out the front door to his house and started walking down Griffith Street. Mac radioed it into Ian, Pocahontas, and Tabitha; as he left his hiding place and fell in, walking a block behind Mr. Moore.

The CID rides converged on the suspect at the same time and he was taken into custody without incident. He evoked his right to speak with his attorney and was transported to Major Crimes, processed and lodged in the Justice Center Jail on Murder in the Second Degree.

A subsequent search warrant on 400 Griffith Street

turned up the murder weapon.

Keyon Moore thought he could possibly game the system with the help of Clarence Darrow, Esquire; but all it really did was slow down the long arm of the law for a beat or two. Mr. Moore was going to have a lifetime behind bars to ponder his gamesmanship and the unwise way he had carried out his numerous threats against Mr. Andrews.

I busted a mirror and got seven years bad luck, but my lawyer thinks he can get me five.

- Steven Wright

CHAPTER NINE

Shortly after that, Mac was doing arrest techniques in In-Service Training in the gymnasium on the fifth floor of the PSB Headquarters building, where he pinched a nerve in his back. He had twisted just right when a shooting discomfort went through his lower back and ran right down the inside of his left leg. It was excruciating pain that left the middle-aged detective hobbled from work.

All cops have bad backs: sooner or later. It was just a matter of time. Wearing a fifteen-pound gun belt as a uniformed officer and sitting for many long hours in a radio car just is a recipe for sciatica pain.

To add to those issues, Mac had always got his children nice sneakers: all he had money left for was twenty-dollar Keds basketball sneakers for himself. He constantly ran three miles in them, totally terminating the discs in his lower back.

Compounding both of those problems, he hadn't replaced his mattress in fifteen years.

The kind orthopedic doctor from Syracuse Orthopedic Surgeons explained that was the reason that he didn't have any fluid between C-4 and C-5, nor in between C-5 and S-1. The doc advised that the swelling would have to go down before he could receive any relief, and when it did, at the very least, he would need new running shoes and a firm mattress.

In the meantime, Mac was laid up on his couch withering in pain, eating hydrocodone like they were M&M's. He didn't convalesce well. After three weeks of being out of work, not doing anything was driving him absolutely crazy.

He couldn't lift weights, he couldn't play softball or basketball, and he certainly couldn't run. It was the first time since he was nine years old that he couldn't play any type of sport.

He would just lay on the couch as involuntary tears streamed down his face from the masked agony.

Joseph was home from college. Mac felt terrible that he was laid up and couldn't do anything with him. It was ironic. He was always so busy at work and didn't have a lot of free time to spend with his kids. Now, he had plenty of free time, but couldn't do anything with them.

On that note, Mac really didn't like to be told what he could and couldn't do with his body.

"Hey, Joseph! Let's go play a round of golf somewhere."

"Dad, do you think that's a good idea? You can barely move."

"I'll be fine. It's a sunny day on a Tuesday in Central New York. We don't get that many. We'll use a golf cart and I won't swing that hard. Make a tee time somewhere and we'll see how it goes."

"Okay, are you sure? Won't you get in trouble if someone sees you playing golf when you're out Injured on Duty?"

"The optics won't look good, you're right. Let's try Roques' Roost Golf Course in Bridgeport. It's not too far, and it's out of the way. We shouldn't know anybody there."

"Okay, Dad. But I think it's going to set you back even more."

"I've got to chance it. I'm going stir-crazy. Maybe it will help loosen some of my back muscles in the process. I've got to try something. I can't keep on laying here."

Joseph drove the Porsche to the golf course that was about thirty minutes outside of Syracuse.

Sure enough, as father and son were gingerly walking to the clubhouse, they came upon Steve, another SPD Second Platoon detective, just getting done with his round of golf.

Mac sheepishly said 'Hi' and kept on going.

One-hundred-to-one odds, it could only happen to Patrick MacKenna.

And, no. It didn't help loosen up his back and Mac could barely swing the club. But, in the end, it was still a nice ride in the golf cart with his son. Joseph, as always, shot a decent score; making it more or less worth the effort and the chance that Mac took.

*

As summer neared its end, Mac's condition showed signs of improvement, only for Joseph to leave for Utica College. Curiously, during his forced hiatus from work; NMI started regularly coming around again to the little white Cape Cod house with the big yard on Milton Avenue.

Mac sensed that she probably had an ulterior motive, but decided not to press her for answers. The mere presence of her brought a smile to his face, as he was overjoyed to have her back.

Then, on a cold October evening when Mac came home from one of his first nights back at Major Crimes, she sprung it on him.

"With or without you, I want you to father a child for me."

Mac figured that this would come into play one way or the other, and he was ready for it.

"If you want a child, then we're going to do it together. We'll start living as a family again," he said, as they snuggled on the couch watching late-night television.

"This house is nice, Patrick, but it's just too small. I always wanted a home with a fireplace. Do you think we could afford to have a bigger house to raise the baby in?" NMI asked.

"Of course. Joseph still comes home from college for the holidays and when school is out of session. I think a bigger house would be appropriate for all of us."

So, it was settled. NMI would go off the pill and Mac would start looking for a new home in the Town of Camillus area. He still had some reservations about her aloof attitude towards him, but maybe all she needed was a new home and to be a mother to change that.

And with that, he contacted a realtor and put up the

charming Cape Cod for sale.

His little voice wasn't so sure, but it was the only thing that hadn't been tried.

This was very unlike Mac. He was throwing caution to the wind, while he ignored NMI's troubling behavior over the past nine years.

But, in the end, he loved her beyond compare: making the leap of faith that he was doing the right thing for all those involved.

*

While he was in the making of big decisions kind of mood, Mac decided he couldn't wait any longer for an NCIS special agent billet to open up in the northeast with the Naval Reserve. He contacted a United States Air Force recruiter in Syracuse about laterally transitioning with the Air Force equivalent—Office of Special Investigations.

He still wasn't getting any younger. Next September he would be forty-two. Kind of old for starting a new assignment in a different branch of the military; and getting dangerously old for going through another law enforcement academy.

But since he was throwing the dice on his personal life, he thought he might as well take the chance on the last passing minutes of time in the reserves and get himself accepted to FLETC before he aged out.

Again, what did he have to lose?

There are risks and costs to action. But they are far less than the long-range risks of comfortable inaction.

- John F. Kennedy

CHAPTER TEN

"**Pay Attention. This is important.** You're a moron!" Sergeant Francis Tucker said.

Mac was standing in the middle of the living room with his ex-partner and good friend. The pair were stooping over the recently deceased body of Jim Day. The twenty-eight-year-old middle class white male was dressed in a black Metallica T-shirt, blue jeans, and gray woolen socks. His current location was lying in the supine position on his plaid couch at 201 Sealy Road Apartment #J1.

Mac was wearing his usual sports coat, dress shirt, tie, dress pants, and dress shoes; while Sgt. Tucker was wearing his now customary sergeant's uniform consisting of a long-sleeved dark blue shirt, dark blue pants, and Bates boots, complete with a black leather gun belt with a gold buckle. The gold chevrons on his collar and sewn halfway down his arms were still shiny.

Mac had been called to the scene of the apparent suicide, where Tucker had also been requested to respond by the two uniformed cops who caught the call.

"But maybe that's the thing that's been missing, Francis. She always wanted children when I first met her. But, I couldn't at the time because of the situation with my first ex-wife.

That could be what made us drift apart. I've tried everything else. I'm still in love with her and completely out of options."

"You see this guy, Mac? He thought he had met the love of his life," Tucker said, pointing down at the stiff on the couch.

"Right after he learned she had been cheating on

him, he took out his Remington 700 bolt-action 308 rifle, pointed it at his heart, and then pulled the trigger. Very romantic, don't you think?"

"Not the same thing Francis," Mac said, as he used his blue rubber gloved hand to pick up the rifle and inspect it.

"What this guy did was dumb. What you're doing is asinine.

"You got extremely lucky to keep your pension from your first wife, and now you're opening yourself up yet again to new litigation regarding your retirement pension," Tucker said, going through Jim Day's wallet.

"You told me she doesn't cook, doesn't clean, and is certainly not affectionate. How is she going to take care of a baby?"

Mac put the rifle back on the floor. He got down on his hands and knees and looked underneath the couch. Blood was still dripping from the gunshot hole where the 308 ammunition had pierced Mr. Day's heart before burrowing through the cushion and frame of the couch. The lead bullet had come to rest on the wooden floorboards underneath.

"Again, maybe because she didn't have what she wanted in the first place meant that she wasn't able to do the other things," Mac said, as he got back up, brushing off his clothes.

"What are you guys talking about?" Sergeant Roderick Dalton said, peeking his head into the apartment from the hallway. The K-9 cop was dressed similarly to Francis, only swapping out the shirt and pants for dark blue BDUs.

"This idiot is getting back together with NMI!" Francis Tucker reiterated, putting down the wallet on the side table.

"Dude...have you lost your mind?!" Dalton exclaimed.

"Will you guys keep it down? I don't need the road patrol cops out front hearing this shit," Mac said in a hushed voice.

He started checking the apartment windows to make sure that they were secure before moving on to the back bedroom.

Francis and Dalton just grinned at each other as Mac walked into the back of the apartment. They knew what they were saying to Mac was pointless, but this back and forth had been going on for as long as they had known him.

"Not only that, but she wants a kid!" Francis said, a little more quietly this time.

"What? No!" Dalton cried.

Mac poked his head back out from the bedroom. "Seriously, you'll wake the dead!"

"Sorry, Patrick. Didn't you tell me that since she's been living at her father's house—rent-free—that she's racked up $8,000 in credit card debt?

"And that her credit is so bad she can't get a new car loan or lease?"

Mac had turned back inside the bedroom and was going over letters he had found there between Jim Day and his former girlfriend. "Yeah," came his muffled reply to his friends in the living room.

"So, doesn't that give you pause? She has a good full-time job. Where's all that money going?" Dalton asked, as he looked at Francis and cocked his eyebrow.

Mac came back out in the living room holding the letters.

"I'm not sure. She likes to go shopping, I guess. Besides, she helped me out when we first met and I was mired in child support payments. It's not a big deal."

"Tell him about her wanting a new house," Francis said, stirring the pot a little more.

"What?!"

"You guys know that house is too small. I've been thinking about getting a bigger one."

"Since when? Your kids are basically all grown and practically out of the house already. And now, you want a new house?" Dalton continued to be bemused.

"Well, not exactly. But after she said she wanted a baby; I thought that would bring the whole thing together for her. You know. Like a grand gesture."

"Oh my God. I think he's definitely lost his mind," Dalton said, reaching up and running his fingers through his thin, brown hair.

Mac walked back into the bedroom with the letters.

"I think we need to initiate an intervention," Francis said in a hushed tone.

"I know," Dalton playfully agreed.

"I can still hear you," Mac said from down the hallway.

Being a very slow day, Sergeant Kylen "Hammer" Duffy walked into the apartment. "Hey slackers! What are we talking about?"

"Nothing much. Mac's just getting back together with NMI, buying a new house, and having a baby," Francis said, grinning.

"For fuck's sake! You're kidding, right?!" Hammer exclaimed. He also was wearing the sergeant's uniform of SPD.

Mac came back out of the back bedroom once more. "For the love of God. Don't you guys have anything else to do?"

The three uniformed police sergeants looked at each other and said in unison, "No, we're supervisors."

"You're killing me, Smalls! I'm working a possible suicide here. Could I get some perspective?"

"It's definitely a suicide," Francis said.

"We all worked Major Crimes, Patrick. Well, besides Dalton, that is. But he was an ET for years before he was a dog cop. So, he knows suicides too."

"If it looks like a duck, quacks like a duck, and walks like a duck..." Hammer said, leaving it intentionally open-ended.

"It's a duck," came the response from the peanut gallery.

"It's not a suicide until I say it's a suicide. It's my case. I'll meet you guys at Coleman's later to discuss my upcoming downfall with NMI.

"Just give me the scene for a little bit. Okay?" Mac pleaded.

"You got it slapper. Hey, you guys want to go and get coffee?" Hammer asked, as his good friends reluctantly retreated.

Finally, peace and quiet with the dead guy.

After another thirty minutes of poking around, Mac conferred with Brian, the M.E. investigator.

Yup. Suicide.

It was slow for a Thursday night at Coleman's Pub. Of course, it was midnight by the time Mac caught up with Francis, Dalton, and Hammer.

Round and round it went, but Mac was undeterred. He was going to give it all he got with NMI. His friends were less than pleased with his decision. They had seen the fallout over the past dozen years or so when Mac and NMI were together. They had valid reasons to be concerned. But in the end, they supported their friend just the same.

Mac left right at last call. He knew NMI was home fast asleep in their bed and couldn't wait to cuddle up beside her.

As he shifted the Porsche into fifth gear on Route 690 westbound, he felt the throaty exhaust as he listened to Toby Keith and Willie Nelson sing *Beer for My Horses* through the sports car speakers.

He knew he had a great set of friends who meant

well; but the rose-colored glasses were on, letting Mac see no downside in being with the one he ultimately loved.

But just before he got back home in Camillus, he remembered the poor soul of Jim Day...

True love is like ghosts, which everyone talks
about and few have seen.

- Francois de La Rochefoucauld

CHAPTER
ELEVEN

At the beginning of 2004, NMI had already become pregnant and Mac was busy trying to sell his neat little Cape Cod on Milton Avenue, while he simultaneously looked for a larger house in the Town of Camillus. He and NMI had been looking, but nothing was really in their price range.

NMI had confided to Mac that she always wanted a fireplace, thus complicating the search just a little bit more. Joseph was off to college, but would be returning in the spring, and this too would have to be considered in buying a new home.

Bridget was still living in Florida with Mac's littlest sister, and Elizabeth was perpetually staying at her mother's home, but these living arrangements could also change and had to be thought of as well.

Trying to purchase a home in the wintertime in Central New York was indeed challenging. Selling a home was downright dreadful.

The area was constantly battered by fierce winds, bone-chilling temperatures, and relentless snow storms. The ground was consistently blanketed in a deep layer of snow, ranging from two to three feet in height. Drifting snow regularly was in the street and on the black tarred driveways.

No one was truly thinking about real estate this time of the year. In the north-east, that was reserved for the spring and summer months.

But Mac was on a deadline. NMI was due in July. He wanted everything to be perfect long before she went into labor. The house would have to be decorated with new furniture. The baby's nursery had to be adorned and put together. There was a lot to do in very little time.

After looking at two dozen homes with NMI with no luck, he found a palatial home in the most desirable neighborhood in the town. The home was a bit out of their price range, but it had been an estate sale that had been sitting empty on the market for over a year. Mac didn't want to get NMI's hopes up, so he made an appointment to see the property one day when she was at work.

Pioneer Farms is an affluent enclave just off the large hill on West Genesee Street before traveling down into the Village of Camillus. The homes weren't built as a traditional housing tract where all the houses were constructed basically the same on equal parcels of land that plowed over the trees and the earth for development.

Instead, each home was built into the landscape utilizing the contours and the mature vegetation growth to enhance each homeowner's property. The structures were all unique in design and used different styles of homes mixed into the development.

Gabel, Colonial, and ranch-style homes were

scattered throughout the expansive neighborhood. Each is exceptional in style and color, with no two looking the same.

Mac grew up in the middle-class neighborhood of Terry Town Heights. Mostly Colonial-style homes in this suburb just outside the city. Their neighbors were cops, insurance executives, teachers, and business administrators who worked mostly in the City of Syracuse. Mac's father was in the hospitality business and barely kept up with the Jones's in the neighborhood.

Pioneer Farms was full of doctors, bankers, and CEOs. The home prices doubled from where Mac had grown up as a kid. It was in stark comparison to his little farmhouse across from Pine Grove Country Club.

Slogging through the snow, Mac got out of his Porsche and walked up to the large white colonial sitting on the corner lot. The realtor was apparently running late, and he decided to walk around the home before she arrived.

The four-bedroom and three-and-a-half-bath home was huge. It had a semi-circular driveway that came off a cul-de-sac, that ran up the front of the home to the two-

and-one-half attached garage on the left side of the home, before continuing up a small hill to the main street. The 2,688 square feet was increased another 1,300 for the finished basement, complete with a wet bar and full bathroom.

The house was set in between mature forty-foot Sugar Maple, White Oak, Eastern Cottonwood, and Blue Spruce Pine Trees. There wasn't much of a backyard. But it was very private, with a ravine sloping to a gorge that had a small babbling brook running down the hill towards the Village of Camillus.

As Mac walked the property, he strode up on the spacious back deck and wiped away the condensation on the sliding glass door window. There he could see the attached four-season room on the back of the home, just off the expansive family room.

His eyes strained to see through the cold frosted glass and the two of the three main elements he knew NMI would covet most of all. A large traditional fireplace in the family room, complete with an exquisite mantle. The four-season room had another gas fireplace. The third fireplace was located next to the bar in the finished basement.

It was the three fireplaces that sold him on taking a look at the affluent property. NMI wanted a fireplace, and he was desperately trying to get her three.

The sticking point was that the estate was originally asking $250,000 for the property. In stark contrast, Mac's little Cape Cod home was being listed for $79,000. He wouldn't even be here if not for the drastic price reduction down to $199,000. That was still outside his reach, but here he was...

A car door could be heard closing around the front of the house. Mac sniffled a bit through his cold and dripping nose before making his way back through his boot prints in the snow to meet the realtor lady.

After a brief introduction, the realtor opened the lockbox, producing a gold key that unfastened the white front door. The front entrance was covered by a portico that held two large white columns on either end of the small brick porch. Think of a miniature White House.

"Where's your wife Mr. MacKenna?" The realtor asked, taking off her boots.

Mac, doing the same, answered, "She's at work. I didn't want to get her hopes up about this place. Matter of fact, I didn't even tell her I was looking at it."

"But why? It's a lovely property. I would imagine with the price reduction, it shouldn't be on the market much longer," she said, as she started walking through the formal living room off to the right.

"To be honest. It might be a little out of our budget, even with the price reduction. How motivated are the sellers?"

Mac looked around at the hardwood floors in the sunken living room as he followed the realtor into the formal dining area, which also had hardwoods. "This is definitely still out of your price range!" His little voice agreed.

The house was un-staged, but still showed well. There would have to be some updates done, Mac noticed, as they made their way into the kitchen, which had an open concept into the family room and the four-season room.

"Oh, they're very motivated! It's been on the market

a while now. I think their original offering was quite optimistic. But the value for your money wouldn't be lost on this property. Pioneer Farms is always in great demand."

Mac nodded, as he followed her around into the half bath, the first-floor laundry/mud room, and into the roomy heated garage. They then went upstairs to see more hardwood in the four bedrooms, and another full bath off the hallway before going into the master bedroom. Again, it matched the rest of the house in grand scale, except for one thing: the master bath was an open concept to the rest of the bedroom. There was no door to separate the two rooms.

Strange, but not a deal killer. There was a raised jacuzzi tub off to the right as you walked in, a separate shower stall, and then the double vanity across from the toilet. To the left was a large area for a king-sized bed, which was well-lit by two skylights in the ceiling. There were also two airy closets to top off the spread-out room.

The realtor droned on and on about the rooms and the possibilities as Mac mostly nodded in agreement. He was overjoyed with what he had seen so far, but was worried he didn't have enough money to make it work. Mac certainly didn't want the realtor to know he was in love with the house, and that he knew NMI would undoubtedly be over the moon with the purchase.

He was lost in his own thoughts on how he could make this work as he followed the realtor down the two flights of stairs into the finished basement.

The lower level, which most certainly was not a basement, was better than Mac had ever seen, with its impressive built-in wooden bar and a third traditional fireplace. The third full bath needed some updating, but the expanse of the rest of the lower level was astounding. There was space to put in a cinema room, a pool table, a foosball table, dart board; and then, there was a completely separate office space off the back of the main room.

"Man cave!" screamed the inner voice. "Family entertainment room," Mac corrected.

At the end of the showing, Mac had devised a long shot of a plan. It was a risky one, but being the dead of winter in CNY, he thought it was worth a shot.

As they were putting their boots back on, Mac said, "I'd like to make an offer at $175,000 with no contingencies."

"Isn't your house still for sale?"

"Yes, it is. But I think my wife would really like this home. I can't go any higher, so that's my best and final offer."

"I'll write it up for your signature and submit it right away, Mr. MacKenna. Let's hope for the best!"

And hope he did.

Two days later, the lady realtor called and said his offer was accepted. Mac joyfully told NMI about the property and the realtor met them at the house to show NMI their new home.

She was as happy as Mac had ever seen her. Financially, carrying two mortgages was going to be tough until he sold his other home, but he thought the tradeoff would be worth it.

Two months later, in March, they moved in and the cleaning and decorating started in earnest. NMI was five months pregnant, and the pressure was on to get everything done.

He co-signed a new lease on a black 2004 Jeep Liberty for NMI and everything was starting to come together.

Mac was reluctant to leave the small Cape Cod home where he had single-handedly raised his three children, but with the start of a new chapter in his life, he couldn't help to be overly optimistic about the direction he and NMI were headed with their unborn child.

Where we love is home - home that our feet may leave, but not our hearts.

- Oliver Wendell Holmes, Sr.

CHAPTER TWELVE

Congratulations, you've been accepted into the United States Air Force Reserve—Office of Special Investigations! The Criminal Investigators Training Program 0505Z and Agency Specific Basic 502 will commence at the Federal Law Enforcement Training Facility in GLYNCO, Georgia from 01NOV04 - 15MAR05.

The letter had come two months after moving into their new home.

So far, 2004 had been packed with new life

experiences for Mac. Besides the new abode, his lateral transfer from the Navy to the Air Force, and the impending birth of his child, he also finally graduated from SUNY Empire State College with a bachelor's degree in Humanities.

Mac's dreams of continuing his education at Onondaga Community College were shattered when he had to drop out because his high school sweetheart had become pregnant. At that moment, his entire perspective on life shifted. Mac never dreamed at the time that he would ever obtain his undergrad degree.

The whirlwind he had been caught up in didn't give him much time for reflection as he physically and mentally prepared for a five-month training program, long away from the palace he procured for NMI.

At his next weekend drill, Mac advised the officers and chiefs of his upcoming departure from the United States Naval Reserve—Defense Intelligence Agency 0797. It was bittersweet. Every one of his shipmates had treated him better than he had ever been in any other professional endeavor. They would be sorely missed.

He was still sitting atop the Sergeant's List, which

again, didn't see any chance of movement in the near future. But work in Major Crimes was still keeping him extremely busy despite all the other changes going on in his life.

Even so, Mac made it home every night to make NMI dinner before she got back from work. The table would be set, and Mac timed it so that he would plate the food as she strode through the door.

He beamed at her every time she walked through the kitchen after her arrival. Mac couldn't have been happier that he had provided NMI with such a grand home, and was taking care of her with a hot dinner every single night.

Joseph had just recently returned home from college. His bedroom in the new house was literally four times the size of his old room on Milton Avenue Mac was just as pleased to have him living with them on his summer break.

After dinner was done, Mac would clear the table; washing the plates, glasses, and silverware; along with the pots and pans before going back to work in the city.

Their old Cape Cod home still hadn't sold. Carrying two mortgages was weighing on him, but Mac was as happy as he'd ever been. He was working towards a better future with NMI and his kids, and it looked like it was starting to finally pay off.

That June, his daughter Elizabeth graduated from high school. Mac and NMI were invited to the ceremony at the Onondaga County War Memorial building. He really hadn't seen his youngest daughter since she decided to go live with her mother and stepfather three years earlier.

It was poignant seeing her walk across the stage, but Mac was still extremely hurt that she had left him the way she did.

On the contrary, it was later learned that his son's GPA was down to a 1.8 Utica College would not let Joseph matriculate for the upcoming fall semester. Unbeknownst to Mac, Joseph had dropped a class in the spring semester, taking only three classes, and still only achieving that dismal grade.

To add insult to injury, Mac had been paying five thousand dollars in cash per semester for Joseph's education. Due to carrying two mortgages, he didn't have enough funds to pay for the last semester. Reluctantly, Mac sold his Harley Davidson 883 motorcycle to pay off the debt.

Joseph was still working part-time at Mully's as a bar back and door guy. But it didn't pay all that well for him to take on that debt.

With most of his kids away from the house, he also decided to sell the Sea Ray Sundancer boat. With an infant, Mac couldn't envision it getting a lot of use for the next several years, anyway. Though he loved boating, doing it without his children just wasn't the same.

Even with these little setbacks and misgivings, Mac was still pleased with the new life and home in Pioneer Farms. Working eighty-hour workweeks between the police department and the military reserves; he still found the time to cut the grass every week and clean the house top to bottom for five hours every month. The chores gave him a sense of ownership of the new property and put everything in proper perspective.

He and NMI had decided not to know the sex of the impending birth. In their minds, as long as the baby was healthy, that was enough. Secretly, Mac knew NMI was hoping for a girl, so he leaned in that direction as well.

On their last OB/GYN visit, the nurse had let her see the sonogram by mistake. NMI thought it might have been a boy. She cried and cried until Mac assured her what she'd seen could've been anything without the medical staff pointing out specifics.

The nursery was completed in a neutral pastel green color. Mac purchased the bassinet, changing table, the dresser, and the rocking chair from Pottery Barn Kids.

The bills were stacking up in his new life, but Mac was certain everything would be all right. Family was the most important thing, and he was running at full speed trying to accomplish this to the best of his God-given ability.

"Come away, O human child: To the waters and the wild with a fairy, hand in hand, For the world's more full of weeping than you can understand."

- William Butler Yeats

CHAPTER THIRTEEN

Meanwhile, one of the most troubling and disturbing kidnap cases at SPD would captivate Central New York; while the men and women of Major Crimes went into overdrive trying to locate and rescue the five-year-old victim.

It was a sunny, cloudless day on the north side of Syracuse when an adorable golden blonde-haired girl traveled over the cracked sidewalks on her red tricycle to see her friend just a couple of blocks away. It was dinnertime, just a little after 6:00 PM, when the girl made her solo bicycle ride on South Carbon Street and came to the four-way stop sign intersection at Hier Avenue. Then it was as if Hell itself had opened up and devoured the girl. She was gone. No witnesses. No video. No leads. Just disappearing into the ether.

While doing follow-ups in the city, Mac heard the 911 Center dispatch the call to units #450 and #452 regarding a missing five-year-old. These calls weren't all that uncommon and most of the time they were rectified in short order. Either the children were found hiding in their own homes, they were out with friends, or they would be found at a relative's home.

What piqued Mac's interest and those of the other Major Crimes detectives was about forty-five minutes later, the road patrol cops were requesting a supervisor to the scene. Then, not too long after that, Major Crimes was requested to the scene as well. Every one of the cops knew that this wasn't good.

This was another All-Hands-on-Deck situation for the detectives in CID. Everyone who wasn't actively with a suspect was summoned to Carbon Street.

"Let's start with a neighborhood canvass. Fletcher,

Atkinson, Pocahontas, and Lou, start banging on doors all around the victim's address. Fry, Cherry, Garner, and MacKenna, start hitting the doors over around the friend's home on Hier Avenue. West, get back to the bullpen and start compiling a list of sexual predators on the northside of the city," Detective Sergeant Bruce Merrill said, giving direction to the semi-circle of detectives on the sidewalk in front of the victim's home.

Carbon Street was starting to look like an ad hoc parking lot for the SPD. Marked cars and unmarked vehicles were strewn up and down the side of the street in every direction. Teenagers on bikes, pedestrians, and people driving their cars in the area all slowed down to try to make sense of what was going on in the neighborhood.

The detectives acknowledged their assignments by heading in the direction of their task, talking amongst themselves as they grouped up and moved in unison. Each had their own portable radios in one of their hands and the cacophony of updated messages by the 911 Center dispatcher on Channel #1 was constant and ever-changing.

While the investigators walked down the sidewalk, each of them took turns asking people they came across if they had seen the little blonde girl on the tricycle. Back and forth, nods prevailed.

The DTs then spread out and started knocking on doors within their assigned area. The response was much of the same. The majority knew of the little girl, but had not seen her this evening.

Neighbors had found her red bike abandoned in a storm drain on the side of the street. No sign of the child. An Evidence Technician took custody of the tricycle in case crucial evidence could be found on it.

Eventually, the newly formed Hostage Negotiation Team responded to the scene and set up in the victim's home. Sergeant Gil Lockhart was running HNT, which was a sub-unit of the Emergency Response Team.

HNT was on site in case a kidnapper called and requested a ransom from the family. This was unlikely, but the bases had to be covered.

The cops certainly knew if someone took the little one, that it was a sexual predator. The coppers also knew that most sexual predators killed their victims shortly after they were of no use to them anymore. A sobering fact for the law enforcement professionals gathered on Carbon Street that day. Of course, that fact would not be relayed to the family.

As day turned into night, other law enforcement agencies were pulled into the search. The Onondaga County Sheriff's Department had sent several marked patrol cars into the city to assist, along with their helicopter unit AIR-1. The sky ship used its infrared capability and searchlight, to search Schiller Park, which was only a couple of blocks from where the girl presumably went missing.

The New York State Police also directed some of its marked patrol vehicles to the city. The north side of the City of Syracuse had more police presence than any other area in a hundred-mile radius.

Still nothing.

Detective Waldon West had compiled a laundry list of sexual predators. The Department of Criminal Justice Services administered New York State's Sex Offender Registry. Only level 2 and 3 sex offenders are listed in the public directory. Even with that caveat, there were over one hundred names on the list.

Since most of them were still under parole restrictions, New York State Parole investigators were called in to assist the Major Crimes detectives in tracking down each and every one of them.

And that's what the CID Third Platoon detectives did after the neighborhood canvasses didn't work out. It was going to be another all-nighter for the men and women of Major Crimes.

Rousting sex offenders on the north side was made easier as a large contingent were housed at the Snowden Apartments located at 400 James Street. The apartment complex had seen better days.

The site was originally a girl's academy that was converted in 1902 by Walter Snowden Smith into a very fashionable apartment complex building resembling the Flat Iron Building in New York City. The large red brick six-story building had a grand walk-up portico with towering white pillars.

But that was not what Mac and his coworkers were

thinking about as they climbed up and down the stairs of the wayward building, talking with one deviant after another; trying to verify where they were at the time of the abduction of the little blonde-haired girl.

Mac knew some of these perverts from his yearlong assignment to the Abused Persons Unit. That had been over eight years ago, and he was still trying to put those memories behind him.

As the sun came up the next day, the search and the subsequent investigation by Major Crimes was no further than they had been when the two uniformed patrol cops showed up at the house the day before. The mood of the investigators was tired and sour as Detective Sergeant Bruce Merrill dismissed them to get some sleep.

The worst was feared.

But sleep was needed. All the men and women would be expected to return to CID by four o'clock in the afternoon to pick up where they left off. They all knew they wouldn't be getting anything that resembled peaceful sleep.

Showered, in new clothes, and sort of rested, the Major Crimes team assembled for the updated briefing in the bullpen of CID—which wasn't much. There had been no leads, no communication from any suspects, and no new direction in which to proceed.

The stale coffee laden aired seemed to be sucked out of the room. The supervisors and detectives alike knew that they were approaching the twenty-four-hour mark and that a bad outcome was all but certain.

Then, as the assembled investigators were looking for any piece of string to pull onto, a very strange thing was occurring. One with very profound morale implications.

Imagine. You were someplace you weren't supposed to be. With someone you weren't supposed to be with. And as fate would have it, you come across a missing little blonde-haired girl who is front page on the local news. And you know your discovery will most certainly ruin your secret and that of the secret of the person you're with.

It is the most quintessential quandary.

If the man just decided to walk away, no one would know. Just him and his conscience. Of course, the child would die.

You be the judge. Was this heavenly intervention or was the universe playing a cruel joke on two people who were given a choice of saving a little one for the sake of them facing derision and ridicule for their original behavior in the first place?

*

A man and a woman who were married, but not to each other, were having an affair. Parked behind an abandoned commercial building in the northeast part of Onondaga County outside the City of Syracuse. The man gets out of said vehicle to relieve himself when he hears small cries from underneath a blue tarp. The tarp appears to be covering a heap of discarded building supplies.

After zipping himself back up, he walks over to the tarp-covered heap, expecting to see an abandoned puppy left to fend for themselves. But to his shock and surprise, as he pulls back the blue tarp, he sees a naked five-year-old little girl. Her head is completely wrapped in silver duct tape and her arms and legs are bound with twisted barbed wire.

Again, you're not supposed to be here. And you're not supposed to be doing what you just did.

Mac's not sure how long the man had to wrestle with his conscience, or even if he discussed it with his cohort or not; but he knows what he found, the dire circumstances of the little girl. He uses his cell phone to call the 911 Center and report what he located.

The world of law enforcement and emergency services descends like a locust on this out-of-the-way lover lane of sorts. The little girl had been physically and sexually abused, and most certainly was left for dead.

But she is rushed to Upstate Hospital for emergency treatment for her injuries. The temperature the previous night had been unseasonably cold, and she was also suffering from hypothermia.

The little blonde-haired girl eventually tells

investigators from her hospital bed the complete story.

While riding her red scooter to her friend's house the day before, she noticed a white car pulling over to the curb. The vehicle door opened, and a Caucasian man emerged. He opened the trunk, saying he was looking for his butterfly catcher, before he quickly closed the trunk, taking her off the tricycle and throwing her into the front passenger floorboard.

She then said as she started to scream, he pulled out a gun and told her to be quiet. Taking her to an unknown location where he sexually abused her. The tiny girl then stated that the man wrapped duct tape around her head and tied her up with barbed wire, leaving her underneath the blue tarp on the heap of construction material, saying that he was going to McDonald's to get her something to eat. That was before dark the day before.

Now, of course, the cops were unsure of the man's story who found the little blonde-haired girl. But eventually, it checks out.

All the law enforcement agencies involved resolve to do their best to limit the man and the woman's moral turpitude with the public in the finding of the young kidnap victim. To Mac's surprise, and that of all the other cops, the press leaves it alone completely.

Now, ladies and gentlemen readers, how does one make sense of this unconventional ending to such a heartbreaking case? Would you have done the same not knowing the projected outcome? Truly, a quandary for the soul.

Be curious, not judgmental.

- Walt Whitman

CHAPTER FOURTEEN

For Mac's last annual training with the United States Naval Reserve, he was sent to Advance Leadership School in Clearwater, Florida. The two-week school was supervision development for Chiefs and Senior Chiefs in the navy. Mac was still only a Petty Officer First Class. He surmised that the command staff at DIAHQ-0797 were tempting him to stay with a glimpse of what the future might be if he stayed with the navy.

The senior leadership had already advised him that

if he stayed, he would most certainly be made a Chief, or that he could apply for a Limited Duty Officer position in the officer ranks. Chiefs were Gods in the navy, and they ran everything. But LDO status meant that Mac could become an officer with more opportunity and responsibility in the Naval Reserve.

Each had its own allure, and it wasn't lost on Mac. But still, his dream was to become a Special Agent. It weighed on him as he spent time in the Greater Tampa Bay area completing his training.

The timing didn't work out quite right with NMI getting closer to her due date. But that was the military. The obligations had to be fulfilled, and this evolution needed to be completed.

Mac was able to secure lodging in nearby Clearwater Beach at the Holiday Inn. The hotel was waterfront and overlooked the Gulf of Mexico. It definitely did not suck.

Every day after school in Clearwater, Mac would come back to the hotel and go for a run over the large bridge that spanned Clearwater Beach and Sand Key. The bridge was built high enough that large, masted ships could come and go without worrying about the clearance as they sailed the waters of Boca Ciega Bay.

The scenery was amazing. Pleasure craft dotted the waterways. Dolphins could be seen from time to time from the bridge mixing with the boats. A large pirate ship carrying tourists sailed out into the sunset of the Gulf of Mexico under a waning moon.

Mac couldn't believe that people actually lived here.

His paternal grandparents had lived not too far away in Pinellas Park. Snow birding back and forth from New York during the winter. But Mac had always vacationed on the Atlantic Coast: Daytona, West Palm Beach, Fort Lauderdale, and Key West.

Now halfway through his stay, on his daily three-mile run, Mac vowed if he ever got any extra money he would try to purchase a property over here in this fifty's era-style beach town.

The pace of life was a little bit slower and not as commercialized as that on the East Coast. Most of the motels on the beach were independently owned mom-and-pop places. The clincher was the crystal-clear turquoise waters and the crystalized white quart sand that made up the expansive beaches up and down the coast.

Someday...

It was probably the nicest annual training that anyone in the military could have hoped for, but he was the only PO1 in the class, which kind of made him an outsider, and, of course, he desperately missed NMI.

*

The two weeks of AT came and went like a dream. Mac was happy to be back home at his new house with a very pregnant NMI and back into his routine of solving cases in Major Crimes.

He got back just in time to join his friends and other members of the City of Syracuse Police Department for the J. P. Morgan Corporate Challenge. The annual 5K road race that brings local businesses together to promote health and exercise while supporting local charities.

The race is composed of over two hundred local

business employee participants that make up the six thousand runners/walkers that run up and down Onondaga Parkway for the three-plus miles before gathering in Onondaga Lake Park for a post-race picnic.

The race had been around since 1982 and Mac had participated with the Syracuse Police Department since he latterly transferred in 1990. It was strictly voluntary for employees to run, but just about all the Emergency Response Team members participated—Mac was still an operator on the team.

"How come you're still in APU?" Mac asked his old sex crimes partner.

"It's for the Monday through Friday—days - work schedule Mac. I can't get that anyplace else in investigations," Katherine "Katy" Hill answered as the two ran side by side in the middle of the throng of humanity on the black asphalt road.

The race had just started with the burst of a loud air horn. Mac had made his way over to her in the chute just behind the starting line.

Katy was built like a runner, being an athletic girl in

her late twenties, standing five foot four inches tall, 115 pounds, with curly long brown hair and delightful freckles. She ran daily and, along with being very attractive, she was married to Mac's good friend from Anti-Crime—Tatum Fuller.

"Where's Tatum? I didn't see him when I got here?" Mac asked. He adjusted his blue tank top Brooks running shirt, which sat over his similarly made red 5" nylon running shorts, as his Brooks white running shoes pounded the pavement beneath him.

"He's back in the fray somewhere. He can't keep up with me," Katy said smiling, as they passed the first volunteer calling out times at the one-mile mark.

"Six-seventeen," the volunteer called as Mac, Katy, and a bunch of other runners sped by.

"Shit Katy! I can't run six-minute miles for distance. I'll catch up with you at the end."

Katy just laughed and gave Mac a wave over her shoulder as she kept up her pace. Mac fell back into the pack for the rest of the race and had a finishing time of 27:58.

Katy Hill had dusted him with a time of 21:33.

Even though it wasn't an actual competition with the cops—it always was.

Large colorful tents of all shapes and sizes were set up over the large expanse of grass in Onondaga Lake Park. Each corporation/business/government entity having its own spot in the park. Folding tables and chairs were arranged underneath with potato and fruit salads, chips, bagels, cookies, hotdog and hamburger buns sitting next to the containers of ketchup, mustard, and relish on top of the tables.

Portable gas grills were manned by members of the command staff of the Syracuse Police Department that continuously turned out a never-ending supply of hotdogs and hamburgers to the hungry runners.

Coolers were scattered around the tents holding bottles of water, Gatorade, and icy cold cans of assorted light beer.

Everyone started off at their own tent after the race but eventually commingled with other tents, looking for old friends or possibly new ones.

"Pussy!" Kylen "Hammer" Duffy yelled.

"What I do?" Mac asked.

"You're drinking water...how come you're not drinking a beer?!"

Mac continued his walk from the food table and sat down on a chair next to Hammer, Tatum, Katy, Scott Sutton, Rod Dalton, and Francis Tucker. He put his bottle of water on the grass by his chair leg as he precariously positioned his food plate on his lap.

"My stomach is too riled up after running. If I had a beer, it would curdle my insides. Besides, I have to get back home to NMI. She's due in a month and she's not feeling all that well in this summer heat."

"Okay, we'll let it slide this time, Mac," Rod said with a wink.

Truth was, NMI had immediately become distant after moving into the palace of a house in the great neighborhood. Every single night Mac greeted her as she came in through the garage door with a huge smile, only to have her return it with a blank - get-back stare. She would go directly upstairs to their master bedroom and wash up for ten minutes before coming back down and sitting at the table that Mac had thoughtfully prepared.

This went on for months with Mac thinking he was as happy as he had ever been, until one day he saw it for what it was. Something was going on with NMI and she was shutting him out completely.

After coming home from work one night, he smelled cigarette smoke in the garage and found a wine glass with remnants of red wine in the bottom. NMI was eight months pregnant. This shouldn't be happening, and Mac didn't know how to address it with her. It would surely be seen as an attack on her, and he didn't want to make matters worse. So, he took the glass off the shelf in the garage, and instead of putting it in the dishwasher, he placed it in the middle of the counter.

He had always asked NMI to wait up for him when he came home, but she never did. She used to before they were married, but not since.

To make matters worse, NMI had started to snore like a lumberjack because of the pregnancy. Mac was a light sleeper and had taken up sleeping on the couch in the basement, much to the chagrin of his ailing back.

He went from thinking that he was as happy as he'd ever been, to thinking that he may have made the biggest mistake of his life.

His good friends had tried to warn him. Because of this, he wasn't about to tell them of his misgivings just yet.

So, instead, Mac just smiled, chewed his food, and drank his water, listening to the conversations of his mates; before heading back to his opulent home to sleep alone on the couch in the dark, dank basement.

The one charm about marriage is that it makes a life of deception absolutely necessary for both parties.

- Oscar Wilde

CHAPTER FIFTEEN

He had a procedure done earlier in the day, so Mac was walking kind of gingerly when he made it to the chaotic crime scene on the westside of the city. The brick nightclub was on the corner of Grand Avenue and Delaware Street. The establishment was called Molly's Place; however, the name belied the carnage that had just occurred within its walls.

Mac was working overtime on the First Platoon after his regular four to twelve shift on Thirds. Several midnight DTs had called in sick and Lt. Shelby Steele had authorized him to fill in for four hours after his regular tour. It was a good thing because NMI wasn't talking to him because of the 'procedure.' Mac's little voice reminded him that she really hadn't had any real interaction with him in months anyway, so what did it matter?

The baby wasn't due for another week, so he'd better get the overtime when he could.

Either way, here he was at another homicide scene in the City of Syracuse.

Being mid-July, the bar was packed on this Thursday evening for Ladies' Night when the shooting occurred at 0114 hours. Customers and onlookers were strewn around the side parking lot of the establishment. Some spoke in excited conversations while others just stared at the brick building where it had happened, as red lights from the arriving police cars bounced off the façade in a regular rotation of inflamed glare.

"What have you got?" Mac asked the midnight road patrol sergeant.

The old sergeant was a midnight lifer. When he was first hired in the early seventies, he worked the graveyard shift. When he made rank as a sergeant, he stayed on the only shift he knew. He was a little on the shorter skinny side and had long graying hair that parted on the side of his head and hung low down into his equally graying eyebrows. The boss always wore the same rumpled, dark blue police ball jacket no matter what season was currently upon CNY.

"Hey, Mac!" came the gruff reply. His salt and pepper mustache crinkled as he spoke. The greeting could've been addressing Patrick MacKenna or that of anyone else he encountered on the street.

"One DRT on the dance floor. He took it in the head. Jamaican male that goes by Big Country. Positive ID will have to be made by the M.E. of course, but his moniker should be in the system."

With the first half of the pertinent information relayed to Mac, the sergeant reached into his pocket, pulled out a Marlboro red, and lit it with a blue Bic lighter.

"My guys have the DJ that was working tonight, as

well as some of the bar staff sequestered in the back of their cars. Do you want to talk to them here or have them transported to CID?"

"Nobody saying who the shooter was?"

"Nope. Before rounding up the employees, my guys rousted the patrons. About seventy-five people in the small bar and nobody saw anything."

"Yeah, I figured. Since we have a corpse, we should take the show downtown. This could be an all-nighter." Mac said, thinking that he was getting more than he bargained for when he volunteered to work part of the graveyard shift.

"You got it. My ET is in there shooting film already and the Crime Lab has been notified and is en route," the sergeant said as he slowly exhaled a stream of smoke from his lips.

The Syracuse Police Crime Lab is made up of a sergeant and half a dozen or so Evidence Technicians who eventually make their way to working days in the Crime Lab processing evidence. They administered all homicide scenes and routinely would be awakened out of their beds from home. This would be one of those times.

The veteran sergeant walked away to speak with his officers and give them direction on transporting the bar staff to the building for the interviews. Customers were still standing on the other side of the softly fluttering yellow crime tape as Mac ducked under and made his way inside the bar.

The young uniformed officer guarding the front door nodded at Mac as he made his way into the crime scene. In return, Mac gave him a good-natured grin. He felt bad that he didn't know his name, but he was somewhat new.

There were a little more than five hundred cops who worked for SPD, but there was a constant wave of retirements, new hires, and transfers.

Purses, light jackets, baseball hats, overturned bar stools, beer bottles, and glassware littered the brown-tiled floor of the drinking establishment. The assorted liquid from the spilled drinks created a slippery walking surface, and the broken glass from the discarded drinkware added another interesting impediment. The

ET had placed yellow plastic tags with ascending corresponding numbers next to a shell casing and some of the other personal items still left at the scene.

Mac walked to the bar to take it all in—crunching underfoot as he went, still walking a little bow-legged.

The stale odor of raw alcohol hung in the air as the midnight ET camera clicked and re-clicked his camera. The officer in his dark blue BDUs shot different angles of the carnage on the inside of the entertainment hall. After each flash of the camera light, the sound of the external light source recharging could be heard over Mac's footsteps as he made his way to the main attraction in the center of the dance floor.

Big Country laid on his back with his head turned slightly sideways perpendicular to the floor. The sightless eyes of the stiff were still open, as was his astonished mouth. Words looked like they would have tumbled out if he could have found the breath to make that happen.

His death outfit was pretty typical of the urban environment at the time. Oversized white t-shirt, baggy jeans, and black Timberland boots. Gold chains adorned his neck. He had a cigar tucked behind his right ear, which miraculously stayed there with the bullet to the head and the fall to the ground.

"Any weapon on him?" Mac asked the ET, as he stopped shooting to let Mac get close to the body.

"Not that I've found. But, shoot, there were so many people here when it happened someone could have certainly picked it up if he had one."

Mac nodded, carefully scrutinizing the body with his eyes, only inches away as he reached into his sports coat and removed blue latex gloves, and began snapping them on.

"ID?" Mac asked, patting the front pockets.

"I didn't roll him yet. I was going to wait for the Crime Lab and the M.E. investigator. You good with that?"

"Yeah, yeah. No worries. I'd just like to know exactly who my victim is before I go back to the PSB," Mac expounded, standing back up. Looking around and seeing no telltale signs of any discarded medical paraphernalia lying around. "Rural Metro didn't touch him?"

"No. They walked in the front door, saw all the blood and half his head missing, felt for a pulse, and left. Not much they could've done for him."

Mac nodded carefully, backing on out. "Thanks," he called, making his way to the front door of the bar, taking off the unneeded gloves as he went.

*

Mercifully, two of the midnight detectives met Mac back in CID with the transported bar staff to start interviews.

It was always like pulling teeth to convince people to tell the truth about what really happened. For a variety of reasons; not wanting any repercussions with the suspect or his crew, not wanting to be labeled a snitch, or that maybe the victim deserved it, or the witness was doing something that they shouldn't have been doing at the time, or maybe they were with someone that they shouldn't have been with, the list goes on and on—but, the truth (or what the cops could get of it) always took hours to elicit from people at the crime scene. The DTs understood this and just bided their time until the witnesses tired of the constant questioning and wanted more to go home than withhold the information anymore.

Mac was still encouraged, though, that during his time on the job, most people did end up cooperating, one way or another.

"Humanity hasn't been completely lost yet," his little voice mockingly chimed in.

Big Country was indeed in the system. He had a lengthy arrest record for the sale of narcotics and had moved up to Syracuse from New York City.

After compiling all the eyewitness accounts, it turned out that Big Country had run afoul of local bad guys in Molly's Place and a fistfight broke out. Big Country was fighting two dudes named Tre and Davon when Chills came up with an oversized army coat on and shot Big Country in the head.

Some witnesses were confused because they didn't

actually see the gun. Chills had fired the pistol with the sleeves from the coat concealing the firearm from public view.

The day major crimes squad would go hunt for Chills. Mac and the other midnight detectives took multiple statements and turned the case over to them to make the arrest and execute a search warrant for the weapon.

Daylight streamed through the Porsche on the way home as Mac tiredly drove Route 690 westbound. The good news was since it was 8:30 in the morning, he could sleep in his bed instead of on the couch. The bad news was that NMI was furious with him for having the vasectomy the day before.

She had wanted more children, but after Mac experienced her apathy towards him and the care of the house, he knew his friends were right. He had made a great error in judgment and wanted to make sure that blunder would not be compounded after the birth of their child.

It was a very difficult decision for Mac. He loved NMI more than life, but he had learned very early on the hard way that love is certainly fleeting...

At my age you don't go into fatherhood lightly.

- Rod Stewart

CHAPTER SIXTEEN

Mac sat rocking back and forth in the wooden rocking chair, staring at the newborn baby wrapped in pink. His daughter attempted to open her cobalt blue eyes, but the illumination of the room apparently prevented her from doing so.

Warm tears streamed down Mac's cheeks. He was still dressed in blue scrubs as he held the tiny bundle of joy. Mac's feelings were mixed. He was overjoyed to have a daughter and to be alone with her just after her traumatic arrival. But he also felt awful that NMI wasn't the one holding her.

The delivery had been a hard one. NMI was in labor at the hospital for nearly forty hours. She had gone into the infirmary on her birthday, but hadn't delivered the baby girl until two days later with an emergency C-section.

Mac had been with her the whole time. Even though it certainly was no picnic for NMI, Mac had to deal with his own demons going back to his first marriage. Wife #1 had hidden a pregnancy from Mac and had a full-term miscarriage that was quite traumatizing for the couple.

From that time forward, Mac found it uncomfortable to be around expectant women. However, that all changed when NMI became pregnant. He was excited to have another child and all the possibilities that came with that. Obviously, a little shine came off the experience with the lack of affection from NMI.

It was all brought back with this hard delivery. After more than thirty hours, the medical staff had induced labor to try to move the procedure along. At one point, one of the nurses had Mac take one leg while the nurse took another; trying to assist with the breaching of the baby. This was horrible to be a part of. NMI was in great pain and totally exhausted by the never-ending birthing exercise.

To make matters even worse: every time she pushed, the baby's heart rate would drop dramatically. Eventually, she was rushed into the operating room and an emergency C-section was performed.

Mac sat at NMI's head while a light blue surgical barrier was set up at her waist so the doctor and the nurses could perform the operation to save the baby's life. He stroked his wife's long brown hair and wiped away the sweat from her brow, as the medical staff literally wrenched their daughter from NMI's body.

His wife's physique would twist and cavort with every tug and pull on the baby. She shouted, "What's going on? Is my baby alright? What's happening?!"

Mac fought back tears as he tried to comfort her. "Everything is fine, dear. They're almost done. You're doing great. They're almost done."

This seemed to go on for an eternity. Then the married couple could hear the cries of their baby from the other side of the barrier.

He stayed with his wife until the doctor said, "Mr. MacKenna would you like to hold your daughter?"

Mac and NMI hadn't known the sex of the baby until that very moment. NMI burst into happy tears upon hearing the news. She desperately wanted to have a daughter, and that dream had just been granted.

He watched as his daughter was washed up, weighed, and tested; before being swaddled up and handed over to him. Mac walked the baby back over to NMI so that she could see her daughter, but she couldn't hold her until the medical staff could put her back together.

"What are we calling her?" Mac asked.

"Katherine. Her name is Katherine," NMI sputtered through her tears.

So, Mac was instructed to take his newborn daughter into the next room and wait until NMI could be wheeled in to be with them. Here he sat with the unending tears, the mixed feelings, and his beautiful daughter trying to look up at him as he assured her with his voice that everything was going to be okay.

To a father growing old nothing is dearer than a daughter.

- Euripides

CHAPTER SEVENTEEN

Three short months later, on Halloween, Patrick MacKenna drove to the Federal Law Enforcement Training Center Glynco campus located in Brunswick, Georgia. FLETC, as it was commonly known, sits in Glynn County on the southeastern part of the Peach State. The training facility is midway between Savannah, Georgia and Jacksonville, Florida. The federal facility is a small city unto itself.

FLETC was founded in 1975 after the closure of the

Naval Air Station Glynco, which was an operational naval air station from 1942 until its closing in 1974. NAS Glynco started as a military airwing housing and deploying dirigibles during World War II. The blimps were used for coastal monitoring of hostile submarines off the eastern seaboard, as well as protection of military and commercial sea assets as they traversed the coastline. It wasn't until the late 1950s that the lighter-than-air ships were replaced with fixed-wing aircraft at the base.

To give some scope to the aptitude of FLETC: it is the headquarters to all other federal training centers located across the United States and sits on 1,600 acres that host modern conventional facilities such as classrooms, dormitories, and administrative and logistical support structures, including a dining hall capable of serving more than 4,000 meals per day.

Additionally, Glynco boasts 18 firearms ranges, including a cutting-edge indoor range compound. Along with extensive, multifaceted driver training ranges, there is a physical techniques facility, explosives range, fully functional mock port of entry, and numerous other buildings that contribute to the entire federal training.

Included in the facilities is a 34-building "neighborhood" practical exercise area. Each house is fitted with video cameras to document a wide range of practical exercises. Inside the classroom buildings, you'll find a range of special-purpose areas, including a library, interviewing suites, mock courtrooms, computer forensics laboratories, and other workrooms specifically designed for fingerprinting and identifying narcotics.

Within Glynco's physical techniques complex, there are mat rooms, classrooms, weight rooms, a gymnasium, and an array of other cutting-edge facilities spanning over three acres, all designed for training and fitness.

The number of federal agencies that participate in the training at FLETC is dizzying.

Of course, Mac was there to attend special agent training for US Air Force Office of Special Investigations AFOSI, but here are the alphabet soup of acronyms for the other agencies represented at the conservatory: AIDOIG, AMTRAK, AMTRAK OIG, AOUSC, ATF, BEP, BIA, BLM,BOP, BOR, CBP, CDC, CIA Police, CIAOIG, CIAOS, CLEC, CNCSOIG, DCISOIG,

DHSOIG, DIA, DOCOEE, DOCOIG, DOCOS, DODCNIC, DODDLA, DODNGA, DOEHSS, DOEOIG, DOIOIG, DOI-OLES, DOJOIG, DOLOIG, DOLOLMS, DOTFAC, DOTOIG, DSS, EDOIG, EPACID, EPAOIG, FAA, FAMS, FDA-OCI, FDICOIG, FEMAOS, FINCEN, FPS, FRS, FWSL, FWSR, GPOOIG, GPOPS, GSAOIG, HHSFDA, HHSOIG, HUDOIG, HUDPSD, I&A, ICE/ERO Academy, ICE/HSI Academy, ICE-OPR Academy, IRSC, NASAOIG, NCIS, NGA, NIH, NIST, NMFS, NNSA-OST, NPS, NRCOIG, NSA, NZPP, OPMOIG, OSMRE, PFPA, RRBOIG, SBAOIG, SDOIG, SI, SSAOIG, TIGTA, TREASOIG, TSA, TSA/FAM, TVAOIG, TVAP, USACIDC, USAI, USBP, USCG -CGIS, USCG-MLEA, USCIS, USCP, USDAAPHIS, USDAOIG, USFS, USM, USMS, USPP, USPSOIG, USSC, USSS, VAOIG, USDAFSIS.

Combine these agencies with the International Training Division, which hosts students from other partner countries from all over the world, and you can see that Glynco was indeed a metropolis in the Georgia countryside.

The Criminal Investigator Training Program is a fifty-nine-day basic school for all personnel in the special investigations course, regardless of agency affiliation. Each Partner Organization has its own criteria regarding being accepted into the organization. Once selected, each recruit must attend and pass the CITP program of instruction that fulfills all the basic criminal investigative training requirements necessary for responsible and competent job performance.

Instead of focusing on a particular agency, the program covers general knowledge, skills, and abilities that every investigator should possess. In addition to traditional law enforcement skills, today's criminal investigators must be well-versed in human behavior, modern technology, cultural sensitivity, law, and other interdisciplinary approaches. This wide-ranging expertise is crucial for effective law enforcement in various situations.

Designed exclusively for full-time law enforcement agents or officers from the Partner Organizations (PO), this program offers specialized training to enhance their skills and knowledge. Recruiting and designating employees for training is the responsibility of each PO, ensuring the highest standards are upheld. Once the individuals have been selected, the organization arranges for them to be sent to FLETC, where they undergo training. Before arriving for the training program, attendees must ensure they meet their agency's recruitment standards and the FLETC Physical Performance Requirements.

Mac had received a copy of the CITP classes for the next couple of months, which covered the prerequisites, before going on for several more months of agency-specific add-on training for AFOSI.

CITP Syllabus/Curriculum

Behavioral Science

- Cross-Cultural Communications
- Cognitive Interview
- Interviewing for Criminal Investigators
- Suspect Interview
- Farina Interviewing

Counterterrorism

- Operations Security (OPSEC)
- Improvised Explosive Devices (IEDs)
- Terrorism
- Aircraft Countermeasures
- Weapons of Mass Destruction
- TSA Regulations: Flying Armed

Cyber

- Introduction to Mobile Device Investigations
- First Responders to Digital Evidence
- Electronic Surveillance Techniques
- Conducting Investigations in the Cyber Environment

Driver

- Non-Emergency Vehicle Operations (NEVO)
- Skid Control
- Cognitive Driver Training—Crash Avoidance
- Emergency Vehicle Operations Course

Enforcement Operations

- Use of Force
- Human Trafficking
- Officer Safety and Survival
- Active Threat Response Tactics
- Basic Tactics

Firearms

- Law Enforcement Handgun
- Firearms Safety Rules and Regulations
- Law Enforcement Shotgun
- Reduced Light for Semiautomatic Pistol
- Down / Disabled Officer Course
- Judgment Pistol Shooting (JPS)
- Live Fire Cover Course
- One Hand Survival Techniques
- Tactical Threat Engagement
- Law Enforcement Skills and Fundamentals Incorporating Training Ammunition (NLTA)

Investigative Operations

- Continuous Case Investigations (CCI)
- Criminal Investigations / Case Management
- Execution of a Search Warrant
- Informants
- Description and Identification Process
- Authentication of Identity Documents for Law Enforcement Personnel
- Operational Planning
- Documentation / Report Writing
- Surveillance
- Undercover Operations
- Radio Communications
- Controlled Substance Identification
- Basic Law Enforcement Photography and Video
- Prisoner Processing
- Basic Physical Evidence w/Questioned Documents
- Recognition of Clandestine Labs
- Investigative Information Sources and Financial Analysis

Leadership Training

- Ethical Behavior and Core Values

Legal

- Officer Liability
- Courtroom Testimony
- Constitutional Law
- Federal Criminal Law
- Courtroom Evidence
- Federal Court Procedures

- Fourth Amendment
- Use of Force (Legal Aspects)
- Fifth and Sixth Amendments
- Electronic Law and Evidence

Physical Techniques

- Oleoresin Capsicum (OC) Spray
- Baton Control Techniques
- Tactical Medical
- Introduction to Physical Training
- Lifestyle Management
- Physical Efficiency Battery
- Community First Aid and Safety with
- Control Tactics

All this information swirled in Mac's head as he made the sixteen-hour, one-thousand-mile trek from his home in Camillus, New York, to the Glynco. He had sold the Porsche for a pre-owned black Saab 9000 with a tan interior for his excursion to the federal academy. It was more practical, with extra space for his luggage, plus the Swedish turbo engine was quite sporty.

Leaving his newborn infant behind was excruciating. Katherine was the light of his life with Mac spending every minute with her before work. Even when he got home after midnight, he was the one who took care of her if she cried in the middle of the night.

NMI never woke up at the calls of Katherine's distress, which was alright with Mac. He would climb out of bed and change her diapers before spending time rocking her back to sleep in the rocking chair in her room.

Katherine's bedroom was painted a pastel green and themed with lambies. After leaving the hospital, Mac went straight to the Pottery Barn for Kids store in the mall. Buying her a white fluffy soft lamb that was put in her crib. Katherine had been inseparable from it ever since.

As Mac drove straight through to FLETC, his mind wandered back to her room and the feel of her in his arms. He hoped NMI would adjust to waking up and taking care of her, but unfortunately, she didn't appear to be changing from her ambivalent state towards him, nor, unexpectedly, the little one.

NMI still seemed to be troubled by some unforeseen glimmer, disappearing for hours while Mac took care of Katherine on his days off from the PD. It loomed large on the horizon, but there was little Mac could do to uncover what it was, or why it was affecting her.

Something else to add to his troubled mind as he traveled south...

I think that in the cultural imagination, motherhood has a primacy that fatherhood just doesn't; and that's not to say that there aren't many fathers who are active and engaged and for whom that is their life's passion. But somehow, in the imagination, there's something different about maternity.

- Rumaan Alam

CHAPTER EIGHTEEN

The trip had been long but uneventful. As Mac got closer to FLETC, he smelled a scent that he was unfamiliar with. It came upon him in the swamp lands as he drove with the car windows down through the temperate southern breeze, just prior to Brunswick, Georgia. He didn't realize it at the time, but Mac had crossed over into America's paper capitol.

The regional abundance of pine trees was the source for the Georgia paper mills. Mac looked off into the distance across the swamplands and saw tall factories producing a light gray smoke that swirled up into the sky. The aroma that Mac was experiencing was the byproduct of paper and pulp industries manufacturing cardboard, toilet tissue, paper towels, diapers, and feminine hygiene products.

The odor was not unpleasant, just a pungent curiosity that mixed with his regretful thoughts as he neared the finish line on his passage.

Kenny Chesney sang *There Goes My Life* on XM Radio, which took him back to his remembrances.

Besides being away from his youngest daughter, NMI had necessitated that Joseph move out of the home before Mac's trek south. Joseph had failed out of college and had only been working part-time at Mully's since his unceremonious removal from higher learning.

Mac was disappointed in Joseph's lack of responsibility in his studies and concerned about him only working part-time in a bar, but was far from asking him to move out of the MacKenna homestead. Unfortunately, NMI was quite insistent, resulting in Joseph grudgingly taking his clothes and moving in with a girl he knew.

It created a divide between father and son, but Mac still thought he could save his marriage, and more importantly, the raising of his little daughter, if he caved in to NMI's demands.

"It's a fool's errand. You know that, right?" his little voice chimed in, as he watched the paper mills in the distance.

"Yeah, yeah, yeah," was all he could reply to the voice in his head.

Twenty-two years after the birth of his first daughter; the country singer's song lyrics resonated more now than ever. Sure, two decades earlier, Mac thought his world was coming crumbling down on him after the news that his high school girlfriend had become pregnant. But it sort of worked out in the end. Although, very unconventionally.

Mac was hoping for a more orthodox ending, as the melody indicated in the later verse for his daughter this time around. The showing of tough love for Joseph was regrettably part of the plan to try to get NMI out of her melancholy funk.

A short time later, Mac was woken out of his revelry at the sight of the main gate at Glynco. Time to try to put those memories aside as he was directed to the Visitors Center to check-in. His head would have to stay in the game for the next six months as he would have to endure another academy at forty-two years old.

"Yippy!" his little voice exclaimed.

Now Mac had reservations in his little voice for once.

"Great. Just great..."

That little ditty would stay with Mac long after it stopped playing on his car speakers. He was determined to try to live the dream that might have been.

All he could think about was

"I'm too young for this

Got my whole life ahead

Hell, I'm just a kid myself

How am I gonna raise one?

All he could see were his dreams

Going up in smoke

So much for ditching this town

And hangin' out on the coast

Oh well

Those plans are long gone, and he said

There goes my life

There goes my future, my everything

Might as well kiss it all goodbye

There goes my life

- Kenny Chesney's

There Goes My Life (Excerpt)

CHAPTER NINETEEN

Lodging at FLETC was dormitory style, with Mac lucking out and getting assigned into one of the newly constructed buildings for students. Since he never went away to college, this was his first experience living in a residence hall full of scholars. Thankfully, each prospect got their own separate room with a kitchenette. There was a laundry on the first floor and common spaces to gather with other students.

It had been eighteen some years since Mac went through the Central New York Police Academy for the

Town of Camillus Police. The apprehension he felt was strangely familiar to that first day so long ago.

The uniform left something to be desired. A baby blue polo shirt with the circle FLETC logo over the left breast, dark blue Dickies work pants, and black boots.

Here he was, a seasoned law enforcement professional, looking like a rook just On the Job. A fresh buzz cut didn't help matters, but the lines on his face told a different story. He had been around the block, and it showed in the furrows on his forehead and the creases around his eyes and mouth.

"Oh, well. Here goes nothing," his little voice said, squirming in Mac's head.

Since there were so many students on the grounds; converted school busses painted all white idled outside the dormitories and shuttled the apprentices back and forth to the classrooms in the center of the campus.

Hefty pine trees dotted the estate, providing privacy from the outside world. Pine straw littered the ground and the sweet smell of sap clung to the warm, pleasant breezes that rustled through the branches.

Mac carried his notebook into the classroom and found his seat. Folded name placards were placed on white plastic fold-out long tables, with Mac settling in behind his. A steady stream of students filed into the expansive room. Glancing around the room, he counted out approximately forty-five name signs.

Of course, most of the faces that Mac focused on when they came into the room were much younger than his. This was to be expected, but it still made him feel ill at ease as people took their seats and started up conversations with others they apparently knew.

Not knowing a soul, Mac just casually listened in as the surrounding conversations flourished. As far as he could tell, most of the recruits were active-duty Air Force non-commissioned officers. There were two captains in the class and a small contingent were civilians. Mac would soon find out that he was one of three reservists, and incidentally, he was apparently the oldest person to attend special agent training.

At precisely 0800 hours, the FLETC Director addressed the classroom and welcomed the students to campus. After the brief remark, he was excused and the

United States Air Force Office of Special Investigations training staff was introduced. There were five OSI special agent mentors for the forty-odd students. The recruits were alphabetically divided up equally among them.

After a morning of orientation as to what was expected of the students and the seemingly endless rules of being on campus, the classmates were released for chow at the base cafeteria.

As they walked across the open-air campus on the way to the chow hall, one of the guys in Mac's group asked, "So, what made you want to do this?"

"Uh, I'm a cop back home in New York. I guess it was a distant dream to think that I could get here someday. How about you?"

"Yeah, you had that look. My name's John. I'm a reservist too and also a cop in Cleveland. I crossed over from the army reserve to get a shot at this as well."

Other members of the group were listening in on the conversation as they strolled over the sidewalks. Further recruits from other agencies dressed in different uniforms roamed among them, coming and going in different directions. FLETC was a busy place.

"I crossed over from the naval reserve. I'm second-guessing my decision now," Mac said, sheepishly smiling back at John as he dodged a coed that wasn't paying attention to where she was walking.

John was older as well, but still about seven years younger than Mac. He was approximately six feet tall, and thin, with dark, shaved hair and hazel eyes. John was good-natured, but there was a tenseness vibrating just below the surface.

"We'll be alright. As I'm sure you know. The first couple of weeks are the hardest. Keep your head down and your powder dry," John said with a wink.

The cafeteria was massive. Everyone appeared to be on different lunch schedules. So, there was a constant bustle of students standing in the lunch lines, sitting at tables, and finally finishing up, taking their green trays in their hands, going to the garbage cans, and clearing the refuse on top off, before putting the glassware, ceramic plates, and silverware on the stainless-steel counter to be washed.

Figuring out the eating establishment took a little getting used to. There were different lunch lines spread out inside the dining hall. Some were for the featured meal of the day. Some were for fast food, like hamburgers and French fries. While still others were for desserts. Civilians wearing pristine white uniforms manned the cafeteria, cooking at the grills, serving food from the counters, and cleaning up as the day progressed. They were all very nice and smiled at the constant parade of apprentices before them.

The workers did this all day. Breakfast, lunch and dinner. Seven days a week. It was quite a large operation to behold: serving thousands of meals a day.

The next nuance was figuring out a place to sit. There were large dining spots segregated all around the inside of the colossal restaurant on steroids. As expected, the alphabet soup of agencies all sat huddled together in different regions of the hall. It didn't appear to be assigned, but they all grouped together at the tables after they received their sustenance from the overly-polite staff.

Mac's OSI group wasn't any different. They all stood

in the same lines with their sub-groups and waited for each other before picking out a table that was turning over with another group leaving.

Just like at the police department and in the navy: there were all types of people represented from society at the OSI academy. Black, brown, yellow, and white. Straight, gay, and bi. Single, married, and divorced. Just about everyone was represented equally according to the outside percentage of the population.

During lunch, everyone's bios were discussed and shared with the group.

Included in Mac's subset group with John was Vanessa. She was a recent college graduate who had come on board through a special program at the university to be a civilian special agent. She was twenty-two years of age with dirty blonde hair, on the shorter, stockier side, with an infectious smile.

Heidi was also a civilian who came from the private sector to be a civilian special agent. She was in her later twenties, 5' 6" tall, medium build, with long dark hair, chestnut eyes and a mischievous grin. Heidi had an undergrad degree and her husband was already in the military in the enlisted ranks.

Erik was one of the two active-duty captains from the Air Force in the group. He was not what one thought of when one thought of an officer in the military. Erik was a prankster that loved to have a good time. He could be fleetingly serious, but he was constantly on the search of an epic time. Erik was from Philadelphia and checked in with dark curly hair, being around six feet tall, and in good overall shape for a late twenties' male.

Jonathan was prior enlisted Army who had been assigned to NATO in Serbia. He was a cheerful, astutely religious, bespectacled young male in his mid-twenties, of average height and weight.

Justin was enlisted, six foot three, rail thin, with sandy brown hair parted on the side and had a quite comfortable ease about him as he spoke. This matched up with his southern German background and manners.

Larry was also an enlisted, active-duty NCO, who was short in stature, bald, and brooding. Like most of the other Air Force enlisted; he was prior Security Forces.

Likewise, so was Naomi. She was of Asian descent, 5

feet 7 inches tall, with an athletic build and silky long jet-black hair. Naomi had a quiet intelligence about her and was deeply driven to succeed in anything she pursued.

There seemed to be a natural progression of those who came from Security Forces to aspire to the OSI special agent ranks.

The United States Air Force Security Forces are the ground combat force and military police service of the US Air Force. The USAF Security Forces were formerly known as Military Police, Air Police, and Security Police at various points in their history.

As they finished up their meals and headed back to the classroom, a bond had started to take hold amongst the sub-set groups in the Air Force Office of Special Investigations Criminal Investigator Training Program. These forged alliances would carry over into the specialized training portion of the academy and, most likely, friendships for life.

Mac had started out apprehensive on his first day at the center, but was comforted by the allegiances of his comrades as they started their shared goals together in this strange and confusing place.

The finest lesson I've learned with age is that all I need is a small team of comrades who inspire me, try not to judge me, and remind me when I'm judging myself.

- Lake Bell

CHAPTER TWENTY

Soon, the recruits fell into the routine of the FLETC learning environment. Some instructors were better than others. During a segment on undercover operations, the OSI special agent the Air Force had brought in clearly had never worked undercover, but faked his way through the presentation. The older cops in the class caught right on to this. Mac especially, since he HAD worked as a primary undercover Task Force Officer for the DEA.

"...but he seemed genuine in his delivery," Vanessa

responded when Mac addressed his small unofficial cohort of friends.

"In his bio when he introduced himself, he never explained how and when he might have worked undercover for OSI, or any other agency for that matter," Mac explained.

"Isn't that a secret or something?" Heidi interjected.

"No, it's not. Being a cop in Cleveland, our undercover officers would share things with us all the time after an operation was done. It's only during the case that methods and sources are kept quiet for the safety of the undercover," John said.

Mac shared a perceptive look with John.

"Yeah, this guy didn't share anything that would make him an authority on this subject. Plus, he gave bad advice," Erik, the active-duty air force officer that came from Security Forces, agreed.

"When I was working undercover, I always looked in mirrors, or reflections in windows, to see who might be behind me. I also never sat with my back to the door. He was saying the opposite of that. If you did that, then the bad guys would think you were a cop.

"That's complete bullshit. Bad guys are constantly jumpy. Looking all over the place so that they could rabbit if someone tries to shoot them, steal their stuff, or arrest them," Mac added.

John and Erik nodded in approval.

The classroom had cleared out for a short break and random other students were intently listening to the conversation. The cops weren't trying to stir things up, but they wanted to set the record straight in case one of their fellow students was chosen for an undercover assignment.

Just then, Mac caught their academy advisor lurking in the doorway. He seemed displeased with what he was listening to and left immediately after being found out.

Knowing that the academy advisor didn't have enough time On the Job to know shit from Shinola; Mac knew some sort of retribution was surely in store for the cops of the group.

Many of the other FLETC instructors were excellent and Mac discovered a newfound sense of learning.

There were classes on behavioral science, financial analyses, and cybercrimes that kept his interest in the program up. The rest of the basic law enforcement curriculum was mind-numbing, though. It was like being a senior in college and then repeating your freshman-year studies.

Before they knew it, the recruits were through their basic training and were moving on to the advanced part of AFOSI course-specific training. Only a couple of candidates didn't complete the basic course. Though all of his friends made it through.

Mac had flown home on the weekends once a month since arriving at FLETC. He missed his daughter immensely, but his relationship with NMI was practically non-existent. Phone calls from Mac weren't answered during the month and seldom returned. Therefore, the trips were bittersweet. Something was obviously going on with her, although at this time Mac feared it was much worse than he originally surmised months ago while she was pregnant.

Meanwhile, with the training half over, the routine would get a little better. The recruits were issued new dark blue polo shirts with the AFOSI crest displayed on the right breast and tan 511 tactical pants. They were no longer at the bottom of the barrel on campus. There was most certainly a hierarchy amongst the agencies; with AFOSI near the top.

During this time, Mac's subgroup inherited a new member. Tony was a tall, good-looking, dark-skinned, thirtyish male with an athletic build. He was in the Air Force Reserves and was able to skip the FLETC basic course because he was already a special agent for the Drug Enforcement Administration.

He had over ten years with the DEA and meshed easily with fellow civilian law enforcement brethren - Mac and John. Unfortunately, this furthered the divide with the class adviser. The three cops had over thirty-five years of law enforcement experience between them. This paled in comparison to the class advisor's three years.

Often, after the class lectures, Mac, John, and Tony would pass on practical experiences they had on the subject to their classmates during the breaks. The class advisor could be seen just outside the doorway stewing over this. There really wasn't a reason for him to be upset. It was good real-world advice from cops who had been there and done that. But because he didn't have that experience to relate to the cohort; the class advisor must've felt threatened in his position at the academy.

Thus, Mac, John, and Tony were being picked apart on small inconsequential nuances at FLETC. During the Emergency Vehicle Operations Course, the cops were admonished for driving too fast and recklessly. Throughout firearms, their class advisor was critical of their firearms quickness on the draw. Defensive Tactics were second nature to them, but they were criticized for not taking it seriously enough. Their narratives on several tests, which were subjective in nature, were critiqued to death, with the results being failing grades.

The cops were winning some of the battles, but the class advisor was winning the war.

Incidentally, Mac lost the Top Gun award in firearms to Tony, who had beaten him by a tenth of a point. In fairness, Mac's SPD duty gun was a Smith & Wesson 4505. Tony shot the same SIG Sauer P229 at his full-time job with the DEA. Still, losing to Tony stung a bit since Mac was on the SWAT team after all.

Even though Mac was past middle age when he entered the federal academy, he still excelled in the physical fitness exams at FLETC. He enjoyed the long runs through the extensive and winding trails that circled through the towering pine tree forest. Mac, John, and Naomi were always leading the way, and it was an unofficial race among the three of them as they breathed in the deep scent of the forest.

One day, instead of organized PT, the class was able to play a pick-up game of basketball in the abundant gymnasium on a full-sized court. This was right up Mac's alley. He'd played basketball since he was a young kid, first playing for the Catholic Youth Organization league at Holy Family Church, then in the driveways of his friends' houses in Terrytown Heights for hours on end. Finally, playing after work in various gyms throughout the City of Syracuse, and on Sunday mornings in an SPD league during the fall months.

However, not everyone at the academy was as familiar with the game as Mac was. One of those was a young active-duty ex-SF enlisted man from rural Tennessee. What he lacked in knowledge, he made up in drive.

Mac was playing point guard for his assembled team. He had brought the ball up court three times, and they had scored all three times. This young man from Tennessee was to guard Mac, and on the fourth time of him bringing it down the court, he decided on a new strategy.

When Mac was at half court with the ball, the Tennessean ran towards Mac at full speed, driving his shoulder into Mac's left shoulder...summarily knocking Mac to the blonde hardwood floor and dislocating said shoulder.

After getting back off the court, Mac's left shoulder hung limp at his side. He was taken to the medical unit within the gymnasium complex. Where medical trainers previously from the NFL and MLB were able to put his injured shoulder back into place.

"Add it to the ever-growing list," his little voice said as he left Sick Bay. "Oh, by the way. How are you supposed to pass the next PEB?"

The Physical Efficiency Battery consisted of a timed

1.5-mile run, a timed agility exam, bench press, body fat percentage, and the flexibility test. This was very similar to the Syracuse Police Department PEB that Mac took once a year.

The exam was given several times throughout the academy. If a candidate recorded a perfect score, they ended up on a plaque in the gymnasium's hallway. For all the students that came through FLETC since its inception, there weren't that many names listed on the plaques.

Mac had aced every category on every PEB test, except for the flexibility test. It consisted of sitting on the ground and placing your feet flat against a wooden box that had a sliding wooden block attached to the top of it. The candidate would have to bend over at the waist and push the wooden block with their fingertips; that would, in turn, slide down a yardstick that showed how many inches it went.

Even with the bad wing, he was still able to max out everything else, but with Mac's prior back issues, there was nothing he could do to improve his score. He was only a couple of inches off from being perfect, but that couple of inches may have well been a foot. It just wasn't happening.

At times, Mac felt like he was faltering at the academy. It wasn't as hard as he thought it would be, but the separation from his daughter, unsupported by his wife, the pushback from his class advisor, not outshining in firearms or the PEB, and now the detached shoulder: it was all starting to take its toll.

His little voice was always quick with a sentiment or two. "There's always tomorrow. Right?"

Ever tried. Ever failed. No matter. Try Again.

Fail again. Fail better.

- Samuel Beckett

CHAPTER TWENTY-ONE

With his shortcomings well documented, when Mac wasn't on a flight home to see his daughter, he would leave base on the weekends and explore the nearby nightlife over in St. Simon's Island, Georgia.

Located in Glynn County, St. Simons Island is a barrier island. The names of the community and the island are transposable, known simply as "SSI", or locally as "The Island". With a population of around 14,000 residents, St. Simons is an integral part of the

Brunswick metropolitan statistical area.

Saint Simons, with its sandy lanes, Spanish moss-laden oak trees, and its connection to poet Sydney Lanier's "Marshes of Glynn," is widely celebrated as the crown jewel of the Golden Isles. What you may not know is that St. Simons is classified as subtropical, meaning that even in winter, Mac could enjoy the island's pleasantly mild climate.

Not knowing where exactly to go, Mac decided to park in the three-hundred block of Mallery Street. Two blocks away, it dead-ended at Saint Simons Pier, overlooking the sparkling Saint Simons Sound.

Mac had always loved coastal beach towns. The wicked winds seemed to whisper and moan through the tall palm trees in the nighttime moonlit sky. They at times seemed like mystical magical places that weren't exactly real.

He supposed it was from watching too many movies growing up. Jaws, The Fog, Goonies, and The Lost Boys, just to name a few. Mac couldn't believe that a small amount of real people lived in places where tourists flocked to by the thousands.

Small old shops from a time gone by era lined the streets. A larger two-story store - featuring lumber, building supplies, and hardware - named J.C. Strother Company - sat among the beach, jewelry, t-shirt, ice cream, and dessert shops.

Mac would normally go by himself, making the thirty-minute ride over to Saint Simons and arriving between nine and ten o'clock at night. Tourists would be seen walking the sidewalks. Couples clasped hand-in-hand, having just finished dinner, strolled peaceably about. Families with their children eating ice cream. All leisurely strolling, seemingly without a care in the world.

The rest of Mac's classmates, and for that matter, all the other FLETC students, were afraid to venture off base. Stories were told of Georgia cops arresting students by the barrel. They didn't care if they were aspiring special agents or not.

He wasn't sure where these stories came from. Maybe they were a form of organized control spread by the FLETC staff themselves. Or, they could, of course, be quite real and told by the students to safeguard any deviant behavior that could dash all hope of graduation.

Either way, Mac theorized, him being a cop himself, that most coppers were reasonable, and they weren't most certainly hunting down FLETC students for the sport of it, especially for leaving the base to enjoy the nearby nightlife in the area.

Besides, he was hanging by a string anyhow. Right?

All kidding aside, Mac was always careful with alcohol. When he was a kid sneaking off into the woods with his friends to attend a keg party, he was the one who didn't drink that much, so as to watch over his companions.

He rarely did shots and had a two-drink-per-hour rule. And yes, he looked at his watch to space them out to half an hour a piece as he went. Third, he only went out for about three hours. Having five to six regular drinks in three hours would keep him under the legal limit on his way back to base.

Of course, he had a lot more rules about drinking that had been previously codified. But these would work while attending FLETC.

FLETC had a bar on base appropriately called the G-Club. However, it was currently closed due to renovations. In the meantime, two doublewide trailers were placed by the athletic fields to take its place. One side had a temporary bar set up in it, with some tables and chairs. The other side was set up as a club-type atmosphere with disco lighting, large speakers, and a darker environment. There were stairs that led up to the doors of each trailer door, and in the middle was a platform between the two sides.

Mac had been there with his core subgroup from the academy on several instances, but the doublewides were kind of depressing. Let's just say the ambience was lacking.

On one of those occasions, though, he ran into an academy instructor from NCIS on the bar side. Mac told him about his time on active duty after 9/11, touching on his time at OCONUS in Bahrain.

"Let me guess. You stayed at the Diplomat Radisson Blu Hotel. Top floor. Last room on the right at the end of the hall."

"Yeah," Mac answered in bewilderment. "How did

you know that?"

"It has been a well-known secret in the intelligence world since they built the hotel. The Ministry of Intelligence from Iran, also known as MOIS, has deep ties in Bahrain. They have been using their intelligence gathering aptitudes at the hotel to spy on the naval base for years."

Mac could feel his jaw slack and drop open. When he could speak, he said, "You mean the US military knows this and we still put people up in that place?"

"Yeah, I agree with you. It's a weird game. But after all, there is limited availability for off-base housing for military personnel and if we just avoided the Radisson, the Iranians would just devise another operation at another hotel. Better to know where it's at and use it against them. Don't you think?"

"Yeah, I guess," Mac said, thinking about all the time he spent in his room. "So, what kind of surveillance did they have on me, then?"

"Twenty-four-hour cameras recording all over the room and, of course, acoustic recording devices. Your internet and phone were most certainly compromised, and you were followed every time you left the hotel."

Dumbfounded, Mac just stared into space, taking all this in.

"But I didn't know anything," Mac protested.

"That was the whole point why you were there. You couldn't have been compromised from an intelligence standpoint. Just think about how many resources MOIS wasted on you."

Still in a fog, all Mac could say was, "But..."

With nothing further coming out of his mouth, the NCIS agent raised his glass and said, "Your country thanks you!"

*

So, with all this outlandish information still on his mind, Mac sat in the upstairs establishment of Rafters on Mallery Street on Saint Simons Island. His prior weekend conversation with the informative NCIS agent still played out in his head.

Coming over to The Island was his little escape from the drudgery and depressing G trailers at FLETC and his imploding marriage.

He let the rum ease into his mind as he watched anonymous patrons on the pool tables and dart boards. A small Irish band called Enter the Haques played up on stage. The smokey bar room swirled with stage lights and neon bar signs. People were enjoying the Friday night activities as Mac pretended to be watching everything but seeing really nothing at all.

Letting everything work its way through his head. He couldn't wait for his time at FLETC to come to an end. He was missing his littlest daughter and that of his older three children. Of course, he missed NMI, but she unquestionably didn't miss him.

Then Mac was confronted by a very dark thought that he didn't really properly analyze at the time that had occurred months earlier.

Homicide was this week's topic at the academy and

something came up that most cops don't investigate that often: poisoning. An investigator could go his/her whole career without investigating a death by poisoning. Their instructors had emphasized that there were ways to kill people that left very little in ways of evidence and that if they didn't know exactly what poison they were looking for; a tox screen on the body by the medical examiner would never pick it up.

Some of these deadly poisons, which were readily available anywhere, were ethylene glycol and methanol. Most commonly found in antifreeze, it is a liquid that prevents the radiator in cars from freezing or overheating. It only takes a small amount of antifreeze to poison the human body and cause life-threatening complications.

Visine Eye Drops is another unassuming lethal poison that is quite common in most household medicine cabinets. The main ingredient is tetrahydrozoline, which is a form of a medicine called imidazoline, which is found in over-the-counter eye drops and nasal sprays. Symptoms were similar to antifreeze poisoning and included:

Altered mental state

Coma (lack of responsiveness)

Difficulty breathing or no breathing

Blurred vision

Blue lips and fingernails (cyanosis)

Changes in blood pressure (high at first, low later)

Change in pupil size

Fast or slow heartbeat

Headache

Irritability

Low body temperature

Nausea and vomiting

Nervousness, tremors

Seizures

Weakness

Mac wasn't sure what caused his mind to knock loose a memory while he sat on his barstool drinking his Captain Morgan and diet Coke with lime. But there it was.

Maybe it was the talk with the NCIS agent the week before bringing him back to his reserve time with the US Navy Reserve, or was it the lessons on poisonings? Or was it NMI's demeanor? Something just wasn't adding up and he couldn't quite put his finger on it, but it was there, just out of touch in the midst of his memories.

Then it hit him like a lightning bolt. A flash of recollection and then an intense internal thought to think if that was entirely possible at all. He was connecting the dots, and more and more they were aligning and dropping into place until he couldn't just dismiss them.

Mac sat there in the middle of a busy Friday night at Rafters; looking at everything, yet seeing nothing at all through the murky smoke of the bustling bar room...

If you prick us do we not bleed? If you tickle us do we not laugh? If you poison us do we not die? And if you wrong us shall we not revenge? -

- William Shakespeare

CHAPTER TWENTY-TWO

It was his last weekend drill with the United States Navy Reserve component DIAHQ-0797. The USNR was quite understanding of Mac's desire to become a special agent with the air force: letting him out of his obligation to the navy, which they didn't have to do.

The Friday night routine before weekend drill was quite routine. Mac would make dinner for NMI and himself before retiring early for his pre-dawn drive to the military base in Rome, New York. NMI was nine months pregnant and the aloofness she projected seemed to amplify daily.

Mac, against her wishes, had just had a vasectomy a couple of weeks before. Giving her a child, a new house, a new car, and a new lease on life was Mac's way of trying to change the dynamic that was keeping them apart. Shortly after NMI got all she wished for; the problems started for Mac.

He went months without a touch from NMI. A kind word or smile was lost on her when it came to him. It was only then that he felt most certainly duped by her designs about getting back together and having a child.

Because of the weight she had put on during pregnancy; NMI had developed snoring at night in her sleep. Mac, being a light sleeper who didn't snore, was given the excuse to sleep on the basement couch for the last four months. Truth be told, it was just an excuse for him not to sleep in the same bed with a person who had become so cold.

So, the strange event that occurred shortly after dinner was odd indeed.

It was nine o'clock and Mac had gotten up off the

brown leather couch in the family room to retire for the evening. He would have to be up by five to shower, put on his naval uniform, and make the forty-five-minute drive to Griffiss Air Base.

"You can sleep in the bed," NMI said from the kitchen table where she was reading a magazine.

Without deviation, Mac had dutifully slept on the couch in the basement for the past six months without fail.

He stopped in his tracks and gave her a curious look.

"I want to stay up and watch a movie on television. I know you probably want some good sleep, so sleep in our bed. I'll just sleep on the family room couch until you get up, then I'll go up to bed."

Of course, there was a television in their bedroom that she used all the time. But Mac, being more tired than usual, said, "Okay, thanks. I'll see you in the morning."

Hugs or kisses were not exchanged as NMI had stopped these long ago. Still, Mac thought it was kind of strange that she was being nice to him all of a sudden.

He made his way to the upper floor of the colonial house, settling into the nice comfy mattress of the king-sized bed in the oversized master bedroom.

Within minutes he was out like a light and navigating himself through dreamworld.

At precisely midnight, Mac woke up with a start. He wasn't sure exactly what the matter was as he tried to clear the cobwebs from his mind. He was disoriented, finding himself in the master bedroom. It had been quite a while since that had happened.

He was also dripping with sweat. Mac was trying to recall if he had been in the middle of a bad dream when nausea overtook him without warning. He stumbled out of bed, holding his hand to his mouth, and darted to the white ceramic toilet in the master bathroom.

On his knees, Mac started praying to the porcelain god. He violently projectile vomited over and over. Remnants of the spaghetti dinner he had prepared six hours earlier visited the inside of the commode.

"What was this?" His inner voice questioned, just

before Mac vocalized.

"For fuck's sake."

Changing positions from kneeling to sitting on the john and letting loose a detonation of diarrhea. His bowels exploded uncontrollably.

Mac's mind was reeling looking for answers. He didn't have an rejoinder for his little voice. He only could concentrate on what end of his body would be positioned over said toilet; altering back and forth. Over and over again.

After three straight hours of this, only clear liquid emerged from his very sore rectum and a very small amount of green bile and specs of blood came from his stomach. He hadn't left the toilet since midnight and it wasn't over yet. His legs were cramping up as he continually changed positions. He was flushing the privy every two minutes to end one process and start another.

Finally, after three hours of this horror, NMI opens the bedroom door and says, "What's going on?"

Apparently, she had heard the non-stop flushing of

the commode and became curious.

"I'm sick and I don't know why."

Mac looked pitiful as his hunched-over, quivering naked form looked over at her from the throne.

NMI stood in the doorway for a few moments and then said, "You must have food poisoning. Let me open the windows up here. It smells disgusting."

And after opening a couple of bedroom windows, she went back downstairs to leave Mac stuck on the toilet in his misery for another two hours. Constantly changing positions and flushing.

Finally, at five in the morning, Mac was able to get away from the john and take a shower to clean himself up from the night's wretchedness.

In his nearly forty-two years on earth, Mac had never experienced anything like that. He figuratively felt near death.

On top of that, Mac had never called in sick to the USNR. He didn't even know where to begin. Eventually, he was able to get ahold of a chief and explain the situation. Mac felt horrible about this as well.

The Navy, and especially all the enlisted, chiefs, and officers at DIAHQ-0797, had treated him better than any expectations that he had prior to joining the military. Mac never got a chance to thank them for this.

He was stricken in bed for another three days. He had to call in sick to work at SPD on Monday as well. He wasn't able to eat and just slept the entire three days.

He couldn't help but think back to what he had to eat on Friday that may have led up to his sickness. Mac seldom ate breakfast or lunch and that was the case on Friday. He didn't know quite how he could've gotten food poisoning from spaghetti and meatballs.

The only thing different was that he didn't have milk with his dinner. They had been out, which was weird because Mac did the shopping and thought he had bought enough for the week. Instead, he had drank a diet Coke with dinner.

The other oddity was that NMI had eaten the exact same thing, and she had been fine. No symptoms at all.

And even though Mac was as sick as he'd ever been; NMI made no attempt to try to get him medical help.

She just told him he needed sleep and wasn't at all concerned with his deteriorating condition.

*

At the time, Mac had chalked that off to her ever-increasing indifferent attitude toward him, but now, as he sat on a Rafters barstool in Saint Simmons Island, he wasn't so sure.

That week's lesson plan on homicide by poisoning, last weekend's chat with the NCIS agent, NMI emotionally and physically freezing him out, and the alcohol starting to take effect: were his thoughts fact or fiction?

Once again, he observed the lively crowd of people bustling around him in the boisterous, smoke-filled tavern on the second floor of Mallery Street on this Friday evening, while he contemplated the various possibilities.

The only difference between the saint and the sinner is that every saint has a past, and every sinner has a future.

- Oscar Wilde

CHAPTER TWENTY-THREE

All that reminiscing was a moot point since graduation was rapidly approaching, and Mac had already purchased first-class tickets for NMI and his infant daughter to attend the graduation ceremony in March. Of course, Mac had never flown first-class, but that didn't stop him from extending the grand gesture to his wife and youngest child.

He was hoping all his supposition the other night on Saint Simons Island was a product of his imagination. Mac thought that if he just kept trying,

NMI would find her way back to him. He had gambled all in with her, hoping that it would pay off someday.

In the meantime, with classes winding down at FLETC, the students could see the finish line and they were starting to relax a bit. Mac, John, and Tony had weathered all the class advisor could throw at them, but it became readily apparent it would be hard for him to fail out the experienced cops without some blowback coming back on himself.

So, Mac found himself chaperoning once again as Erik—the active-duty commissioned officer of the group—ordered a limousine to pick up the subgroup of friends from the G trailers for an excursion to Jacksonville, Florida on a Saturday evening.

Mac, John, Tony, Johnathan, Larry, Heidi, Vanessa, and Naomi were all huddled around each other.

"Erik, where are you taking us?" Heidi asked, sitting on a picnic table next to the baseball field.

"Jacksonville," Erik said, taking a pull on his Coors Light beer bottle. He was already a little buzzed.

The team-building softball game had concluded

some time ago, and the socializing had been underway for a while now.

"Jacksonville?" Vanessa repeated.

"What's in Jacksonville?" John inquired out loud, nursing his own beer bottle.

"Strip club," Erik replied.

Mac, John, and Tony shared a troubling look. As cops, they knew nothing ended well at a strip club. The rest of the de facto group wasn't thrilled about the idea either, but didn't want the birthday boy going down to Jacksonville by himself.

A luxurious, long white limousine picked the aspiring special agents up in style, ready for their hour-long journey to the gentlemen's club. Erik made sure to grab the remaining ice-cold beers for the journey. As the others nursed their bottles and made idle conversation about what would happen after graduation, he relentlessly hit it hard.

Erik and the active-duty personnel were going back to their original bases and were being assigned to the OSI detachments there. Vanessa and Heidi were waiting on their civilian assignments, although they knew they would most likely get their preferred posting. Mac, John, and Tony would go back to their civilian careers in law enforcement and be obligated to the one weekend a month, two weeks a year commitment in the reserves.

The nearest OSI office for Mac to drill at was in New York City. He had learned that Detachment 426 in lower Manhattan was located in the Jacob K. Javits Federal Office Building at 26 Federal Plaza on Foley Square in the Civic Center neighborhood of Manhattan.

Mac further learned that AFOSI Detachment 426 was mainly stood up with retired and reserve special agents from NYPD. Their main mission was Protective Service Operations in the metro New York City area. PSOs consisted of dignitary protection of senior officers in the United States Air Force. This was an important assignment, especially during wartime.

Scores Jacksonville is an upscale gentlemen's club on the southeast side of downtown Jacksonville, Florida. As far as strip clubs go, it was better than most.

The small group of friends exited the limousine and made their way into the dark confines of the pleasure palace.

Late teens and early twenty-something girls dressed in upscale bejeweled lingerie paraded around the inside of the red velvet interior of the nightclub in their high heels. Pulsing music vibrated through the FLETC cadets as dazzling colored lights ricocheted off the customary mirrored disco ball hanging above the main stage.

A small brunette in a school girls' outfit was just starting her routine on the stage when a bleached blonde cocktail waitress in curls wearing a sexy cowgirl outfit came up with a tray to Erik.

"Do you want a Jello shot baby?"

"Um, sure. Why is it in a tube?" Erik said boozily through slit eyes.

"Because, sugar, I have to blow it into your sweet mouth," the veteran waitress said with a coy smile and a wink of her pale blue left eye that was covered by a long, extended false eyelash.

Heidi, Vannessa, and Naomi rolled their eyes and continued following the hostess to the provided table next to the main stage; while Mac, John, Tony,

Johnathan, and Larry stayed with Erik and looked on in mild curiosity.

"That'll be ten dollars, honey!"

Erik dug deep into his pocket and produced a twenty-dollar bill. "Keep the change," he said with a slight burp and a crooked smile.

The cocktail waitress scooped up the money with one hand and put it in her brasier. While holding the circular brown tray with one hand, she took her other hand, picked up the tube, and put it in her mouth. Erik cautiously leaned over the tray and put his mouth on the other end of the small plastic hollowed tube.

Mac and his cohorts heard the cowgirl exhale into the tube connecting the waitress and the sightly inebriated Erik; sending the green gelatinous glob into his awaiting mouth.

The gag reflex on Erik was legendary.

His eyes instantly watered up and his facial features queued into a man with an urgent sense of panic. With his airway compromised, the primal urge to breathe took over and the involuntary reflex catapulted the green, slightly used Jello shot back into the cowgirl's overly made-up face.

The brown circular tray crashed onto the highly polished floor of the nightclub. Plastic tubes clicked off the floor as the tray spun around on its own.

The cowgirl cocktail waitress seemed to be frozen in time.

Mac's little voice interjected into his head, "I would've thought that it would have stayed in a ball of Jello."

But it hadn't.

The waitress was covered in small but abundant pieces of green goo. It was on her attractive face. It was stuck in her oversized black eyelashes. It was wedged into the bleach-blonde curls of her hair. Some lime specks adorned the brim of her white cowgirl hat.

Erik had turned her mute. It seemed after thirty seconds that she was still trying to process the entirety of the simple transaction.

"I'm so sorry!" Erik blurted as he stumbled to try to pick up the remnants of the Jello shooters on the floor and place them on the wayward tray.

Mac and the boys couldn't contain their collective laughter. They tried to stifle it as they left their comrade in clean-up mode, making their way to the table with the girls.

A hulking bouncer eventually came over to try to regain decorum in the upscale gentleman's club. He took the tray with the assorted tubes from Erik with one hand and directed the frozen cowgirl with the other to the back of the house for cleanup.

A shaken Erik came and sat at the table and exclaimed, "You would've thought that they should have known that would have happened!"

The table of aspiring special agents roared with more laughter.

Their swift time together was just about done, but these memories they shared for the past five months would undoubtedly stay with them for a lifetime.

I did work in a strip club, but I didn't strip. I danced, and I became very popular.

- Maya Angelou

CHAPTER TWENTY-FOUR

NMI and the baby flew in the following week. Mac was elated to see them. He gave them both big hugs, taking them from the airport to The King and Prince Beach & Golf Resort on Saint Simons Island. This enchanting ocean front resort boasts 192 guest rooms, each uniquely designed with its own captivating decor and breathtaking views. From snug rooms in the main building to expansive two- and three-bedroom villas and resort residences, the accommodations cater to all preferences. The resort is situated right on the beautiful beachfront of the Golden Isles, allowing guests to soak up the sun and enjoy the pristine, sandy shores.

At great expense, Mac had again tried to impress his wife with a luxurious hotel for her and Katherine's stay the night before graduation. Pale yellow buildings topped with red terracotta roofs decorated the sprawling property, which were offset by the Atlantic Ocean's turquoise surf in the background. The sound of constantly crashing waves could be heard ubiquitously around the resort.

Nestling their slumbering baby on the luxurious king-sized bed in their opulent suite, the married couple stealthily retreated to the expansive en suite. In the dimly lit room, their bodies intertwined with fervor, their hearts pounding in sync as the sweet aroma of desire filled the air. It had been several long months since they had indulged in such passionate intimacy.

After a luxurious dinner, the family settled into their well-appointed accommodations for the evening slumber. Graduation was the following day and the couple with the child would be leaving Georgia for the long trip back to their home in upstate New York.

For the occasion of graduation Mac selected his best Brooks Brothers classic fit wool checked 1818 suit in navy, a freshly starched white J. Crew Bowery button-up dress shirt, a burgundy Tom Ford silk tie, and a pair of Gibbons cap toe Johnston & Murphy dress shoes in mahogany. Of course, taking into consideration Mac's financial status, all this fine gentlemen's wear was obtained at a steep discount. But none were the wiser.

NMI had packed a very summery flowered print dress from The Limited that came down just below the knees and white strapless sandals.

Katherine was adorned in the latest toddler fashion from Pottery Barn for Kids.

Graduation itself had the pomp and circumstance of a public coronation. The morning weather was in the mid-seventies, with only small puffy clouds dotting the dazzling Azul sky. The lofty pine trees swayed with just a hint of breeze as the candidates and their families gathered outside the administration building for the ceremony.

One by one, Mac and his fellow mates walked across the dais to receive their diplomas, and more importantly, their credentials as a special agent. The creds, or cred pack as they're commonly called, is what derived their authority as a criminal investigator for the United States Air Force.

Smiles beamed across the faces of the new special agents as they saw the creds for the first time; thrusting them out for husbands, wives, boyfriends, girlfriends, and other family members to see. It was a proud representation of the accomplishment of the past five months of determination.

The ceremony was over by noon. Hands were shaken, backs were slapped, and hugs were embraced with their fellow students, with the earnest promises of staying in touch and the well-wishing that accompanies such departures.

Mac's memories of his time at FLETC would probably be different from his younger peers who had attended the federal training facility. He was certainly impressed with the overall makeup of the Federal Law Enforcement Training Center, but was slightly disappointed with some instructors that had certainly slipped through the cracks to teach the students. Of course, his associates, besides the other cops, wouldn't have had the life experience to make the disparity.

All in all, it was another hurdle accomplished late in life and Mac couldn't wait to see what lay before him in the United States Air Force—Office of Special Investigations Reserve.

*

The happy couple seemed to be getting along just fine as they packed up from their one-night stay at The King and Prince for their car ride up the East Coast. Mac once again loaded up the Saab 9000 for the return trip with his family.

His little voice thought it would be nice to have company on the ride. Katherine was such a good baby and seemingly never cried or fussed. NMI enjoyed commenting on the scenery and talking about what updates she was looking forward to making on their home, as they made their way north on Interstate 95.

Mac just smiled through his Ray-Ban Clubmaster sunglasses, looking at his wife as she prattled on without a care in the world. It had been a very long time since she seemed interested in being in his company.

"Maybe absence does make the heart grow fonder?" Mac's little voice interceded.

Perhaps, Mac thought, as he continued listening to her go on and on. He couldn't contain his exuberance and found himself laughing with her as she found new subjects that enamored her on the ride.

They agreed to stop in Norfolk, Virginia, to break up the fifteen-hour-long trip. Katherine was an amazing traveler, but that would be pushing the limits of the most perfect baby.

Ironically, while Mac was in the Navy, he had never stepped foot on a naval vessel. But now that he was in the Air Force, he was visiting the world's largest naval station.

Naval Station Norfolk is a United States Navy base in Norfolk, Virginia, that is the headquarters and home port of the US Navy's Fleet Forces Command.

The MacKenna family arrived at the Norfolk Waterside Marriott just before eight o'clock in the evening. The hotel was in the heart of downtown and overlooked the Elizabeth River.

Subsequently checking in: Mac, NMI, and baby Katherine went back downstairs to the Capo Capo, Italian Steakhouse for a late dinner. After being cooped up in the Saab for seven hours and eating fast food, it was nice to be relaxing in an upscale bistro.

By the time the trio was done with their meal, a gentle breeze had picked up, carrying with it the scent of night-blooming flowers, prompting them to retire to their room for the evening. Despite the progress they had made, they were only halfway through the trip. They decided to extend their stay in Norfolk by another day to explore the city and ensure they were well-rested for their morning walking tour.

Sleep came easily on their plush King-sized bed. A bassinet was brought into the room for the baby and all slept peacefully through the night. Mac was content to play big spoon as NMI curled up against him under the freshly laundered linen.

Mac sensed harmony and contentment, with no doubts or uncertainties clouding his mind. He felt an overwhelming sense of gratitude as he looked around at his family, cherishing the precious moments together.

The Norfolk Waterside Marriott was only steps away from the Nauticus Waterfront Maritime Museum, and the USS Wisconsin BB-64. The weather wasn't as temperate as Georgia, with the family having to bundle up for their stroll in the chilly portside town.

Mac pushed Katherine in her stroller as NMI dutifully walked by his side as they toured the waterfront. The indoor Nauticus museum was quite comfortable as they toured the exhibition hall with all things nautical.

Again, Katherine was happily seen and not heard. She gooed and gawed at her parents from time to time, but was rather content to be wheeled around inside and out.

Bringing a baby stroller onto the USS Wisconsin BB-64 seemed impractical enough to keep Mac's streak alive. He would have to wait another day to board a navy ship.

The MacKenna's found a small family-run restaurant featuring American cuisine for an early dinner. Once over, they walked back to the Marriott to end their tour of downtown Norfolk.

Mac and NMI watched some television while Katherine was content in her bassinet, before retiring themselves, breaking from their sojourn and continuing on home to Central New York.

The next day they were safely at their house in Camillus.

Being home, Mac felt an overwhelming sense of relief wash over him. The last four days spent with NMI and baby Katherine felt like a dream, filled with laughter and joy. Graduation had come and gone, leaving behind memories of a brief but encouraging road trip and layover in Norfolk, which hopefully foreshadowed good things to come.

Special Agent Patrick MacKenna was as optimistic as his Gaelic soul would ever let him be.

"Being Irish, he had an abiding sense of tragedy, which sustained him through temporary periods of joy."

- William Butler Yeats

CHAPTER TWENTY-FIVE

The month back working as a detective in CID for SPD flew by and before he knew it, Mac was queuing up for his first stint as a special agent for AFOSI in the reserves. The assignment was in Lower Manhattan with AFOSI Detachment 426, as expected.

Mac was in charge of making out his own itinerary through SATO. SATO offers travel services for U. S. military and civilian government agencies, such as travel management, expense tracking, and hotel programs. He was pleasantly surprised that on the government dime, he was able to book a direct air flight through American Airlines while also being able to book a room at the Embassy Suites by Hilton New York, Manhattan, located in Times Square.

He dressed in a dark blue pullover J. Crew polo with Brooks Brothers khaki dress pants, and cordovan Johnson & Murphy loafers. Mac wore his AFOSI-issued sidearm in a paddle holster on his right hip, which he covered up with a canary yellow Helly Hanson windbreaker.

Packing up his black garment bag with his dark blue suit, three white dress shirts, and accompanying three solid subdued ties, Mac was once again melancholy about his home life. NMI had almost immediately become aloof, leaving him once again sleeping on the couch in the basement of the opulent home on the well-manicured cul-de-sac. Shoving his dress shoes into the front zippered part of the bag, he audibly sighed as he looked at his baby daughter playing on the bed watching him pack.

Mac had taken Katherine to the pediatrician for a wellness visit and learned that NMI had not had any of her childhood shots administered. The poor kid was left getting two shots a piece in each arm. The affable baby cried and cried in Mac's arms at the doctor's office. It was just one more thing on the long list of many. However, her ambivalence was now affecting his youngest daughter.

He lifted Katherine off the King-sized bed in the master bedroom with the skylights above, shouldered his garment bag, walked down the flight of stairs, and gave her to her mother in the family room. Mac kissed them both on the forehead and drove himself to Hancock International Airport for the short plane ride to New York City.

Since 9/11 occurred air travel had changed immensely. At one time, family and/or friends could escort passengers right to the gate and see them off at takeoff. Now TSA controlled all pedestrian travel within the airport; restricting non-flyers to the entryways of the facility.

Mac was enthusiastic to fly armed. He had never had the pleasure prior to 9/11, and now that it was even highly restrictive, it felt even more special. The Syracuse

Police Department controlled the local law enforcement at Hancock. Cops, mostly working on overtime, would man checkpoints and patrol the interior and exterior of the air facility.

"Hey, Patrick! Where are you off to?" Sgt. Rod Dalton asked as he approached the checkpoint.

"Hey Roderick, I'm on my way to the city for the reserves. I need to sign the book," Mac said to his friend.

The "book" was an antiquated system reserved for cops and special agents flying on duty and carrying firearms.

Dalton, a K-9 sergeant, gave TSA security a nod and was able to check Mac into a small back room that held a large ledger book where Mac produced his AFOSI orders and displayed his cred pack.

Even though they were good friends on and off the Job, procedures were procedures.

"Nifty!" Sgt. Dalton said in an amused, mocking tone as he checked Mac's creds.

"Very funny Rod. How many hours of airport time do you have this week?"

Dalton: "Sixteen. Eat your heart out. Any word on the sergeant's list?"

"Nope. At this point, I'm probably going to die on the list."

As Dalton signed his name on the ledger next to Mac's, he said, "Well, hang in there my friend. I hear that they're going to hire a new class and do promotions within the next six months."

"Yeah, yeah, yeah. I've heard it all before," Mac said as he picked up the garment bag and made his way to the gate.

Dalton just chuckled and went back to his post. Having a bomb detection dog made his presence at the airport on his time off almost mandatory.

As Mac made the long walk to the gate, he thought of the tall, thin, good-natured cop. Dalton worked a lot of hours and didn't have a care in the world. He had never been married and didn't have any children. Dalton wanted for nothing. His house, newer Ford 150 pickup truck, and two jet skis were paid for. He had a healthy stock portfolio and a nearly six-figure bank account, but Mac still worried about him just the same.

Even though Mac had four children, an ex-wife, an aloof current wife, and all the worry and misery that came from that, Dalton's lack of those things somehow made Mac uneasy about Dalton's future.

Ultimately shrugging it off, he continued on his way to the gate.

Mac reached the podium for the jetway and discreetly told the flight attendant that he was armed. She escorted Mac down the corridor into the cockpit to meet the pilots. All standard operating procedure with armed cops traveling the friendly skies.

*

The dignitary was Admiral Tom Anderson. Another irony for Mac. He had transferred from the Navy to the Air Force and was constantly being reminded of his old service.

Admiral Anderson was in charge of the United States Northern Command, as well as overseeing the

Northern American Aerospace Defense Command. This put him under the umbrella of the United States Air Force and granted him a protection detail from AFOSI.

Being the commander of NORAD gave him the foreboding assignment of having the launch codes for nuclear missiles for the Department of Defense.

"Yeah, he's a big deal, and this is a huge big-time assignment," Mac's little voice commented as he was being briefed in the hotel about personnel assignments within the PSO detail.

The admiral had one full-time special agent assigned to him, along with a half dozen adjunct officers, of all different ranks from the navy. Mac learned that one of the officers was a pilot for the infamous Blue Angels.

Patrick MacKenna was standing in the presence of some awesome individuals.

But the special agents from the New York City detachment were equally impressive. The office only had approximately six full-time civilian agents. The majority of those were young, fit, and well-educated. The SAC was a retired NYPD commander who had also been an AFOSI reservist for twenty years.

The rest of the AFOSI reservists were just as old and salty; full-time NYPD cops with assorted backgrounds. Detective Seargent Mickey Quinn was the most intriguing. A bomb technician who was present at Ground Zero on 9/11 and lived to tell the tale.

The old-time copper and sometime special agent was small and lithe, like a welterweight boxer. His weathered face cracked as he mischievously smiled through nicotine-stained teeth, telling yarns of war stories from long ago.

Legend had it that Quinn would routinely go by the Hells Angels Club House. A six-story lightly gargoyle Renaissance Revival apartment building with a first-floor brick façade at 77 E. Third Street: pissing on the front gate, as he yelled insults at the criminal bikers inside.

The occupants apparently were well aware of the crazy Irish cop and preferred to ignore the sacrilege and slights he offered during his late-night sojourns through the East Village.

The Protective Service Operation Day started at 0600 hours, with the itinerary of the day and the personnel assignments. Four late-model armored Chevrolet Suburban's were used; all with blacked-out windows and adorned with blue and white government license plates.

The detail met with Admiral Anderson in the hotel's lobby and quickly escorted him to the awaiting vehicles just outside the front door of Embassy Suites.

The schedule for Friday and Saturday was jam-packed. The reason for the NYC trip for Admiral Anderson was mostly ceremonial.

Mac started out driving one of the support SUVs containing some of the admiral's support staff and the cache of heavy weapons. Caution was set to the wind as the four-vehicle caravan snaked through the already crowded midtown Manhattan streets on the way to 30 Rockefeller Plaza for an early morning television interview at NBC studios.

The most bizarre thing to Mac was that the motorcade didn't stop. Not for anything. They, Mac included, drove like madmen through Gotham from one location to the next. That meant driving through red lights, around NYPD traffic cops directing traffic, or going up on sidewalks when traffic began to back up. NYPD was quite used to all the protection details that came to town and just took it in stride.

Being the FNG, Mac was left with one other special agent guarding the SUVs as they sat just outside an adjacent entryway. It wasn't glamorous, but once these vehicles left the super-secret bat cave, they couldn't be left unattended for obvious reasons.

After an hour or so there, the entourage continued to the next stop, which was in lower Manhattan for a meeting at the New York Stock Exchange on Wall Street. Mac was once again left with the government vehicles as he stared at the galloping bronze bull statue out front.

"Huh, I thought Wall Street was a lot bigger than this," Mac's little voice pined.

He wasn't wrong. The area was a lot smaller than it looked on TV. It was also true when they next went to the Headquarters of the United Nations building.

"Or maybe New York City is so big...everything

seems so small," Mac's little voice offered once again.

Mac concluded he wasn't wrong. NYC was busting at the seams of constant people and vehicles in motion. Everyone was in a hurry to get from here to there. AFOSI just took it to the next level.

While he and his partner waited outside the UN, another special agent picked up some sandwiches, chips, and sodas for lunch. The other agents rotated out of the circle of protection, one at a time, to do the same.

Another meeting was attended in lower Manhattan at a nondescript office building before finally traveling to Central Park for a dinner at the famed Tavern on the Green. The admiral was meeting with some serious movers and shakers.

Tavern on the Green had started out as a building in Central Park to accommodate sheep in the 1880s before being transformed into a restaurant shortly after the end of prohibition in 1934. To honor that rich history; the long red awning to the entryway exhibited two standing sheep holding a sign displaying the name of the fine dining eatery for all to see.

Admiral Anderson, who was still wearing his white cover, military dress white uniform, complete with ribbons and metals, made his way past the restaurant's ever-present doorman, who also didn't disappoint in his dress. Adorned in a shiny black top hat, white tuxedo coat, and black cropped riding pants that tucked into shiny black long riding boots.

It was quite a sight to see the admiral walking down the carpet underneath the awning surrounded by the protection detail and his adjuncts, as the doormen graciously held open the door to the red brick, gray-roofed tavern accented with white trim. And yes, people did stop and stare at the procession as they entered the grounds.

The first day of the NYC PSO ended at 2200 hours when they tucked the admiral back in at Embassy Suites after his Tavern on the Green engagement. An hour later, Mac and the other agents secured the Suburban's in the non-descript government garage before returning to the hotel to get some sleep.

Getting up at 0500 hours on Saturday for another equally brutal seventeen-hour day was not easy for anyone on the PSO detail.

This time Mac was assigned to be traveling in Admiral Anderson's vehicle with the dignitary himself. The admiral was quite cordial. Asking Mac about his background and, upon learning about Mac's prior service, inquiring about his time on active duty in the Navy.

During Saturday's excursions to Battery Park and ferry ride to Ellis Island, Mac was once again assigned to car-watching duty. Which held true to their trip to Ground Zero, where the admiral toured the hallowed grounds for the first time.

From there, Admiral Anderson had been invited to a soiree at the Ritz Carlton in Central Park by an aristocratic lady that had ties within the New York City government. She was alone and the admiral graciously offered her a ride to the event uptown.

As Mac sat in the front passenger seat of the Suburban, he couldn't help but overhear the older lady say to the admiral, "My, isn't it so nice to have these guys giving you rides all over New York?"

The aristocrat was referencing the special agents of the PSO detail for AFOSI.

Very politely, but firmly, Admiral Anderson answered with a smile on his face, “Ma’am, these gentlemen are very highly trained special agents of the United States Air Force. They are armed and protect me with their very lives.”

With that, the woman blushed a bit, and prattled on a bit about the war effort and how grateful she was to the United States Military.

It was a very long weekend by the time Mac flew back home late Sunday night. They had gotten up early the next morning to escort Admiral Anderson to his G5 at the airport. He was heading back to Washington, DC, for a meeting with the Joint Chiefs of Staff.

Mac couldn’t help but like the New York City special agents and the hospitality they showed him. If possible, he even like Admiral Anderson even more for his kindness and the clarifying comment he made to the aristocratic woman in the back of the SUV.

Mac lamented that Protective Service Operations

weren't for the faint of heart. His first PSO had gone off without a hitch. He was quite earnestly looking forward to playing special agent again next month in Gotham.

My dad was the town drunk. Most of the time that's not so bad; but New York City?

- Henny Youngman

CHAPTER TWENTY-SIX

While Mac was off playing special agent, the City of Syracuse was experiencing a troubling trend of late-night commercial robberies of restaurants and bars. Two masked African American males armed with handguns had hit four places over the weekend. No one had been hurt yet, but all the cops knew: it was just a matter of time.

The robbers would bide their time, waiting until just after closing hour, when only the staff remained in the building. After rounding up all the employees, they would lead them into the room containing the safe, where they would seize any United States currency they came across. The bad guys would menacingly instruct the staff to wait for a nerve-wracking ten minutes before contacting the authorities, or else face the threat of returning to inflict harm.

Captain Walsh assigned the detectives of CID Third Platoon mandatory overtime to try to apprehend the successful crooks. When the DTs got done working at midnight, they would partner up with one another in unmarked CID rides for stakeouts all over the city. Each pair would take a Remington 870 shotgun with them.

Detective Sergeant Bruce Merrill and Detective Corey Barlow would divvy up assignments to adequately cover the twilight restaurants and bars in the City of Syracuse. There clearly weren't enough coppers to cover every late-night establishment in the city.

It wasn't an exact science. Basically, the detectives were watching the busier places in their sector. The common-sense reasoning was that the bad guy duo would risk more for a greater reward.

Mac was teamed up with Pullman for these late-night assignments. He was Mac's junior in age and On the Job by seven or eight years; and had recently been assigned to CID on the evening shift.

Pullman was of moderate height and weight, being just over six feet tall and wearing his two hundred pounds well on his stocky frame. His bright hazel eyes nicely highlighted his dirty blond shaggy hair and accompanying wolfish grin.

The younger detective was likable enough but was part of the Detective Sergeant Corey Barlow clique of junior detectives. Mac didn't play favorites between his bosses and didn't really have a problem with the informal clicks in the department; as long as they didn't get in the way of good police work.

Mac and Pullman were first assigned to the Armory Square business district, where most of the late social life occurred.

Mac backed the non-descript black Oldsmobile Cutlass into the shadows of the gravel parking lot at the corner of West Fayette Street and South Franklin Street. The foliage near the back of the lot made them even harder to see from the lighted city streets and the businesses they were watching.

This hiding spot gave the DTs a view of the main thoroughfare of West Fayette Street; as well as Mulrooney's Tavern, Kitty Hoynes Irish Pub, The Stoop, and Zoo Station.

As with most stakeouts, it was just a long exercise in staying engaged with the mission while trying to stave off boredom and tedium. Both detectives were familiar with the game. Passing away the hours with idle chitchat about internal gossip within SPD.

"What are those two guys doing?" Pullman asked.

It was just about the 2:00 AM closing time when two men were seen leaving the front door to Zoo Station and going partly down the side alley of the building.

Mac pulled out the binoculars from off his lap and took a look. There was just enough ambient light shining from the streetlights into the alley to see facial features.

"Um, that's Luigi, the manager. I don't recognize the other guy though," Mac said, as he tried refocusing the glass on the two subjects.

"What are they doing?"

Mac: "They are...they are...making out."

"What? Are you kidding me?! I didn't know he was gay!"

"Me neither," Mac said as he lowered the binocs and placed them back on the seat.

It was kind of weird. The cops were the good guys, but now and then, they felt like they were doing something wrong. Like playing peeping tom or stalking innocent people.

A weird dichotomy, but it was the J-O-B.

Night after night, Mac and Pullman got different assignments throughout the city, with pretty much the same result.

The crime duo struck a couple of times, but there were only so many cops covering a large number of late-night businesses. It was frustrating, but again, surveillance is not an exact science.

Eventually, Mac and Pullman were assigned to cover Mac's local: Coleman's Irish Bar on Tipperary Hill, known for its lively atmosphere and traditional Irish music. Coleman's had been a familiar haunt for Mac ever since he reached the age of eighteen. It was during Mac's bartending stint for his dad that he first met Peter Coleman Senior, thanks to his father's introduction.

Rosie's Sports Bar -just up the street - had been one of the spots hit by the bad guys. Mac had asked his bosses if he could cover this assignment. Rosie's was owned by the Coleman's, and it was a logical assumption that Coleman's Irish Bar would be next on the list.

Tipp Hill was mostly residential and off the beaten path. Neighborhood bars were sprinkled in between the two-family flats that covered the Irish stomping grounds on the west side of the City of Syracuse.

This also made it difficult to conduct surveillance. The parking lots were well lit. Sitting on the streets under streetlights would identify the pair of DTs whenever anyone drove by the tavern.

With this in mind, Mac waited until after closing and snuck in the back way to the bar with Pullman. Mac had the shotgun and greeted Patrick Coleman—the pub manager, and his barmaid Kimmy.

"Holy shit Mac, you scared the crap out of me!" Patrick Coleman shouted as he saw Mac and Pullman coming out of the back kitchen.

Mac: "Well, we're here to make sure that you don't get robbed for real. How have you been Pat?"

Patrick Coleman and Kimmy were wearing the seasonal uniform of white button-up dress shirt, black tie, black pants, and black rubber-soled shoes.

"Fine, I guess. These late-night stick-ups have us all on edge," Patrick said, as he came over and shook Mac's hand.

"This is Pullman. We're assigned to you guys tonight. We'll stand on the backside so no one can see us through the windows, then we'll walk out when you're all done counting the money and putting it away."

"Thanks, Mac." Kimmy came around the bar, giving Mac a big squeeze around the neck. Kimmy was a hippie child with long, ebony, flowing hair that she tied up with a black ribbon.

"No worries. You guys just close up as usual and we'll stay out of your way," Mac said, holding the shotgun away from Kimmy as he returned a one-arm hug.

Pullman sheepishly smiled at the two. Outwardly seeming extremely uncomfortable inside the Irish tavern.

"Haven't seen you in a while Mac. Where have you been?" Patrick asked, as he returned to the bar top and resumed counting money into stacks.

"I've been busy with the Air Force Reserve. Five months of training in Georgia, a weekend in NYC doing drill, and most importantly, taking care of baby Katherine."

"That explains the absence. Well, your presence is missed!"

Patrick Coleman was a little younger than Mac, with brown short hair and sapphire blue eyes. He was just about six feet tall and thin. His affable smile was the perfect gift to a tender of a bar.

Kimmy generously offered Mac and Pullman sodas from the bar gun while she and Patrick sorted out and counted the cash.

Patrick and Kimmy finished up with their closing tasks around 3:30 AM. Mac and Pullman walked out the kitchen door first to the side parking lot.

Mac: "You know Patrick, you should keep this door locked."

"I know Mac. The employees are constantly coming and going throughout the night, taking out trash and bottles. I'll remind them again about keeping it latched."

Mac gave Patrick and Kimmy both hugs, telling them he'd be in when he could to get a drink and catch up.

With the assignment completed, Mac drove him and Pullman back to the barn, the sound of their tired footsteps echoing in the empty corridor. The usually affable Pullman was strangely hushed as Mac bid farewell to Pullman in the courtyard, setting off for his ride back to Camillus.

*

The following night's overtime shift had been

adjusted. Detective Sergeant Barlow admonished Mac for bringing Pullman into Coleman's Irish Bar and reassigned them to another location for stakeout.

Pullman had used his pull from being in Barlow's click to undermine Mac's seniority on how to conduct the surveillance at Coleman's.

He fumed at the slight, his jaw clenching tightly as he refused to engage in any further car banter with Pullman at their new stakeout location.

Later on that night, the criminal twosome struck Friendly's Restaurant on the far northeast side of the city on James Street. Since they were assigned to the north side, Mac sped to the location of the armed robbery, hoping to catch the suspects as they were leaving the area.

Twenty minutes later: The 911 Center dispatched Shots fired with Injuries from Coleman's Irish Bar on Tipperary Hill.

Mac glared at Pullman as he got the Oldsmobile to warp speed on the highway. Emergency lights flashed, and the siren wailed as Mac put the pedal to the floor.

The trip took less than five minutes as the police car maxed out at one hundred and twenty miles an hour.

The 911 Dispatchers advised that Patrick Coleman had been shot in the upstairs office near the safe and that Kimmy was still on the line with the 911 Center pleading for help.

Mac and Pullman were the first units on scene. Mac didn't wait to confer with Pullman, as he leaped from the skidding car and made his way into the bar through the unlocked kitchen door.

Stainless steel .45 pistol thrust out in front of him: Mac took the back stairs from the kitchen to the third-floor office two at a time. When he got to the landing he yelled, "Kimmy it's Mac...I'm coming in!"

The barmaid was still on the phone with the 911 Center. Mascara was running down her nose as she looked up at Mac from her sitting position on the hardwood floor.

Patrick was lying on the flooring next to her, holding an extremely bloody and destroyed ankle. He grimaced in pain. "I gave them the money, Mac, but they shot me anyhow!"

"Unit #739, we're on scene. One shot in the ankle. ETA on Rural Metro Ambulance?" Mac said over his portable radio.

"The rig is just pulling up out front. They were waiting for the scene to be secure before they made entry." The male 911 Center dispatcher answered.

Mac: "It's okay Patrick. Paramedics are coming up now."

Pullman finally made it to the top of the landing with his own gun out. He looked at Patrick and Kimmy with a hint of shame in his eyes; as he re-holstered his firearm, slowly walking back down the stairs to meet the arriving paramedics.

Mac wasn't sure if Pullman had been scared the night before, or that he simply felt it was tactically unsound to be in the pub while bad guys could be lingering just outside the door, but Mac wasn't interested in what he thought at this point.

The other two DTs—also part of the Barlow click—had apparently left the detail early. On surveillance, you

NEVER left your assignment.

Mac was pissed.

He had been taken off an assignment where he would've protected his friends. The cops who left their posts were never disciplined.

Mac could tell by the look in Pullman's eyes as he made his way back down the staircase that night that he felt a sense of responsibility.

Maybe Mac was upset because he had been on the SWAT team for ten years and felt very comfortable in tactical situations. Or maybe he was more upset because he had been sitting on a supervisor's list for an extended time now and this scene should have never shaken out this way.

"Or maybe, just maybe, you're upset because a couple of friends of yours were terrorized, and one was needlessly shot for no good reason," his little voice whispered.

Regardless, the robberies abruptly stopped after that fateful night. Despite the numerous crimes that occurred during that late-night crime spree, there was never any accountability for those responsible.

Good, better, best. Never let it rest. ‘til your good is better and your better is best.

- St. Jerome

CHAPTER TWENTY-SEVEN

The Joint Chiefs of Staff for the United States Military were the top echelon of martial leadership in the American government. As the advisory body for military matters, the Joint Chiefs of Staff consists of the most senior uniformed leaders within the US Department of Defense, offering guidance to the president, secretary of defense, Homeland Security Council, and the National Security Council.

The following month found Mac once again in New

York City for a protection detail. But this was no ordinary PSO.

AFOSI Detachment 426 was protecting the Chief of Staff for the United States Air Force.

There were five other Chiefs of Staff for each service; Army Chief of Staff, Marine Corps Commandant, Chief of Naval Operations, and the Chief of the National Guard Bureau.

The Chairman of the Joint Chiefs of Staff is a leader of their branch of the military and is appointed by the President of the United States, confirmed through the United States Congress. The Chairman is the president's top military adviser.

USAF General Roger O. Thornhill was in New York City for an exceptional affair. The Chairman and all the members of the Joint Chiefs of Staff were conferencing at an exclusive invite-only think tank symposium.

Mac wasn't familiar with the details, but the special agents and the part-time reservists (NYPD cops) were all in a tizzy. These types of meetings hardly ever occurred outside of Washington, DC.

And again, being wartime, this was a very big deal.

Accommodations did not go as well this time for Mac through SATO.

The New York Yankees were playing a seasoned ending home game against their bitter rival, and Mac's favorite team—the Boston Red Sox. Billy Joel also happened to be playing at Madison Square Garden.

Ergo, there were no good hotel rooms left in the City of Gotham.

The visiting special agent for General Thornhill graciously offered his couch in his room at the Embassy Suites. Mac, not having a clue on what to do, took him up on his offer.

They wouldn't be spending much time in the room anyhow, but Mac still felt awkward about taking him up on his proposal.

Mac flew in Friday night and hooked up with the special agent at Embassy Suites. The PSO was a logistical nightmare, with special agents from all the services meeting at the conference location to provide specific and collateral coverage for all the dignitaries in attendance.

After spending a very uncomfortable night on the couch in the visiting agent's room, Mac was awakened early to the PSO briefing and then out the hotel door to the awaiting caravan of blacked-out armored Chevrolet Suburban's.

He was once again relegated to one of the support vehicles carrying the weapons cache and some of the adjuncts for the general.

The entourage of the five blackout Suburban's left the hotel early with their charges and made the mad dash to a non-descript brownstone on the upper east side.

At the same time, special agents from the other services were doing the same with their esteemed members of the Joint Chiefs.

Of course, all the movements were carefully choreographed. But Mac couldn't help but wonder how all the government vehicles didn't somehow collide in the middle of intersections in NYC while en route to the symposium.

The outside of the unnamed brownstone looked pretty much like the rest of them in New York City. Maybe you had to be a New Yorker to tell the difference from one to another.

But this one held a lavish auditorium in the basement. The only giveaway that something special may be occurring inside of the building was the fleet of Suburban's on the surrounding streets.

Mac mercifully didn't have to guard the SUVs on the street this time. He took his position in the protective ring as General Thornhill made his way in the early morning heat to the front door, and then down to the underground room.

Special agents from the military services were stationed at all the entrances. They also mixed with the exclusive crowd of one hundred attendees in the bowels of the building. This was an invite-only soiree. Although Mac still wasn't sure why or how they were chosen for such an event.

The attendees appeared to be on the older, affluent side of the tracks. Sitting in chairs in the middle of the chamber, they listened as members of the Joint Chiefs of

Staff spoke over an audio system to the crowd.

There was an unknown moderator dressed in a dark suit at the dais. He asked the high-ranking members of the Joint Chiefs about the ongoing war effort, lessons learned, and expected initiatives in the future.

It was pretty surreal. Mac felt this was an all-access pass to the inside workings of the Pentagon on the Global War on Terrorism.

Again, who were these people, and what kind of public relations stunt was this?

Although, no press was invited. All phone and recording devices were confiscated at the entrance to the hall.

Being very new to AFOSI, Mac was resistant to asking his fellow special agents. He figured it was need-to-know, and if they didn't tell Mac, he had no reason to ask.

It was another very long day that went well into the night. The special agents were always on their feet and couldn't afford to relax. They were ultimately responsible for their dignitary. Relaxing out in public was something that didn't happen.

Like before, the special agents were rotated out one at a time, where they were provided with sandwiches, chips, and bottles of water. They ate their sustenance in the expansive kitchen just off the great hall. Kitchen workers hurriedly came and went, preparing and setting up food for the attendees at a buffet.

The aroma of salmon, pasta, and steamed vegetables mingled in the air. Pots, silverware, and dishes clanged together as the special agents took their very brief break in the boiling steam and din of the surrounding chaos, trying to stay out of the way as they quietly munched on their meager meals.

Mac took a few minutes out of his break to once again try to find a hotel room through SATO in midtown. The customer service representative was able to find a single room in an obscure hotel. Not wanting to sleep on the couch again, Mac jumped at it.

Admiral Thornhill was finally escorted back to the hotel at 2300 hours that evening. The Protective Detail was once again exhausted. It had been another seventeen-hour day.

"Oh, by the way." Mac's little voice interceded. "There is no overtime for reservists. You're paid the same as if you worked an eight-hour tour."

"Thanks," Mac muttered as he gathered up his garment bag from the visiting agent's room and made it back downstairs to one of the black SUVs. There was no time to take it back to the bat cave. It would have to be thoroughly gone over in the morning before the next PSO began.

Mac followed his directions to the hotel in the middle of midtown Manhattan. There was no parking garage. That should've been the first sign that something was wrong.

The second one was that there was no lobby. Just a sleepy clerk sitting at a desk in a very narrow hallway. Mac asked the clerk where he should park the Suburban. All he got was a half-hearted shrug.

Going down the hallway was the third indication this was a hotel that Mac should not have booked. He opened the door to his room with a gold key on a large brown plastic key chain and found a single bed in a room the size of a closet. The bathroom was even smaller, if that was at all indeed possible.

Mac threw down his garment bag on one side of the bed and plopped down on the other. He contemplated going back to the Embassy Suites and bunking back in with the visiting agent, but it was approaching midnight and he had to be back up at 0530 hours the next morning to do it all over again.

Instead, he made his way back through the hostel lookalike to the government SUV he had left on the street in a NO PARKING ZONE. With no other alternative, Mac drove the Suburban up onto the middle of the sidewalk and tossed the NYPD parking permit on the dash.

Leaving it on the street wasn't an option. The entire street for blocks prevented any kind of street parking. Traffic would be backed up persistently and the government vehicle was more than likely to get hit and damaged by a gypsy taxi or a rundown city bus.

He was as exhausted as he'd ever been.

"If it's here, it's here," Mac murmured, as he went back to his less-than-desirable room.

It seemed, as soon as Mac closed his eyes, his alarm went off and he was shaving, showering, and putting on a new shirt, tie, and socks with the old suit and shoes. He sleepily made it back down to the sidewalk, where he saw the most bizarre sight.

Throngs of pedestrians flowed around his black Suburban. They were all going in the same direction and the movement resembled that of a swift current going around a large rock in a river.

It was just another day in the life of a New Yorker, but to Mac, it was a wondrous site.

The PSO for General Anderson ended the next day at 1600 hours when they put him on a G5 headed back to Washington, DC.

The general had been just as pleasant as Admiral Anderson the month before. And just like the admiral; he had given all members of the protective detail a challenge coin with his name and command on it.

These PSOs in New York City were proving to be long and arduous days, but the command staff who they were protecting were well worth the mission.

AFOSI Detachment 426 had its own challenge coin. It was enameled in black with a large red apple on one side containing the OSI patch and badge with the gold script AIR FORCE OFFICE OF SPECIAL INVESTIGATIONS—NEW YORK CITY. On the other side of the coin was the Statue of Liberty, being escorted by two special agents with their firearms out, inscribed in silver with DETACHMENT 426—DEFENDING FREEDOM * PROTECTING LIBERTY.

Out of all the coins gifted to him in the military, this was his favorite.

I run from Horatio Street down just past Battery Park City and back. It's amazing to run and see the Statue of Liberty and the ferries coming in. People think if you're not near Central Park, there's nowhere to go, but there's a whole ecosystem happening down here.

- Andy Cohen

CHAPTER TWENTY-EIGHT

"A flush beats a straight every time, gentlemen," Danny the bartender exclaimed, taking both hands to rake in the winnings on the large wooden table.

Stray cigarette smoke from the after-hours game hung just above the table as the tinkling sound of plastic poker chips came to life as the barman stacked his newly acquired wealth.

Mac was back home in Syracuse and playing cards at Mulrooney's Bar just after 0300 hours.

After the late Thursday night shift from CID, Mac, Waldon West, Liam Fletcher, and Zachariah Fry were playing the card game with the Mully's staff. Drinking for the cops and barmen was almost nonexistent. The real allure was a card game called Texas Hold'em.

Jaimee, Mac's good friend from the Navy, had taught the game to the late-night cop patrons and employees of Mulrooney's prior to 9/11, and now that Mac was back home, it gave him something late night to do to relax.

He had been sleeping on the couch in the basement of his impressive home for nearly two years now: he was growing extremely weary of it.

NMI had kept up her aloofness and self-centered dogma since he had been back home from FLETC. Again, he did all the housework of cleaning and washing the floors, dusting the thirty-eight hundred square foot house, cleaning the three and a half bathrooms, taking the garbage out, cutting the grass: as well as food shopping for the household, and his culinary duties every night, setting up the table and clearing and cleaning all the pots and pans.

This combined with his sixty-to-eighty-hour work week, SWAT training, testifying in court, regular overtime, being stuck on cases after midnight in CID, and his once-a-month reserve obligation with the United States Air Force as a special agent—was a little much.

But the lack of affection was leading Mac down a path he didn't want to go. No embraces, no kisses exchanged, and God forbid—no getting naked with the only girl he loved—was surely accelerating a decision he didn't want to make.

Taking care of his daughter Katherine every day before work was the only solace he received within his abode. He loved her more than anything, but something needed to change to bring NMI out of her egocentric fixation.

So, tonight had become somewhat of a trend in Mac's chaotic life. The coppers and the bar folk would sometimes play until dawn, laughing over stories told at the darkened and scarred wooden table in the back booth of the emptied-out bar. Cards would be shuffled by the dealer and thrown out in front of each participant with the assorted players banging their cards on their edges to get them aligned for the furtive look at their fate, before betting or folding in the constantly changing hands of the game.

Tonight, though, a uniformed rookie had slipped between the cracks and made it into the inner circle of veteran cops to play Texas Hold'em.

When the new kid went to the men's room, the conversation instantly flourished with hushed voices.

"Who the fuck let Beuford in here?" Ian asked, looking around at the other players at the table.

"I thought he was with you guys! He's been hanging out here a lot lately." Danny came clean, taking responsibility for the error.

"Come on Danny! You know better. The kid's brand new. Besides, from what I hear, he's already a zero," Zach added, looking toward the men's bathroom door.

"What's a zero?" Double D asked. Double was one of the more popular Mully's bartenders.

"It means he's not doing his job on the road. He shouldn't have made it out of FTO if they're right," Mac said as he looked at his newly dealt cards.

Beuford had a large build, but not in a good way. He was approximately fifty pounds overweight on his 5'11" frame, and his cherub face was perpetually pink from an early onset of hypertension. He was only twenty-one years old but had already acquired the guise of an experienced bullshitter in his short time on earth.

"He told me earlier that his family was friends with the captain in Personnel and that's how he got the job," Liam Fletcher added. "I raise two bucks."

Mac went back and peeked at his cards. "Why would he even want to be On the Job? I'll call Liam's raise."

"Believe it or not, Beuford told me he became a cop to pick up chicks!" Zachary sputtered, spitting out some of his beer in the process.

"Oh, God" groaned Waldon West, amongst the snickering from the rest of the group.

Everyone looked in the direction of the men's room to see if there was any movement.

"By the way, Beuford also heard you were on the top of the sergeant's exam. So, don't be surprised if he's trying to be your best friend. He kisses ass with every gold shield he comes across," Liam added.

"Great, that's all I need. Has anyone told him that the list has been going on five years?" Mac responded.

"Nope. We want to see you squirm," Zach said. "I'll re-raise two bucks."

Mac looked at his pair of twos and a pair of sevens. "I'm out," he said, throwing the upside-down cards into the other discarded dead cards on the table.

The bathroom door creaked back open. The cops and the bar staff tried not to look Beuford in the eye as he came back over to the table.

"On that note, I'm out of here," Mac said, standing up and adjusting his firearm on his hip.

More groans from the table.

"NMI will be up getting ready for work and I've got to watch the baby. Hopefully, she goes down for a long nap or I'm screwed for sleep," Mac added, taking his car keys out of his pocket and ruefully squinting at the lightning of the skies through the large picture window. The portal in the bar's front façade was stenciled in gold:

MULROONEY'S.

Mac's early departure only disrupted the rest of the card players for a moment or two, as they went back to calling the hand in play.

Driving home on Route 695 Mac listened to *Boulevard of Broken Dreams* by Green Day, trying to make sense of his recent choices in life. Little did he know a maelstrom awaited his arrival back home.

NMI had apparently heard him enter the downstairs garage door into the house. She was upstairs, banging cupboards in the bathroom with her displeasure.

"Good, maybe we're getting somewhere," Mac's little voice said.

"Now's not the time," Mac mumbled back, as he took off his dress shoes and made his way upstairs to his daughter's room.

Not surprisingly, Katherine was sitting up in her crib in her flowered onesie, smiling at Mac as he slowly opened the door to her room. He put her on the changing table to remove the wet diaper and dress her for the day. NMI could still be heard banging her hair dryer and other items intentionally off the bathroom counter.

Once dressed, Mac held a smiling Katherine in his arms as he walked by the slightly cracked door to the master bedroom; hoping to temporarily avoid the wrath of NMI and make it to the kitchen so that he could get her fed in peace.

But the bedroom door swung violently open before they had a chance to make it to the stairs.

"Where have you been?"

"Playing cards at Mully's," Mac said, continuing to the stairs and hoping to avoid another disagreement with NMI.

"Bullshit! You were with a girl!"

Mac chuckled, "I wish."

Mac's little voice: "Probably not the right thing to say, Romeo."

He had made it to the top landing of the stairs when NMI rushed him from the bedroom and violently pushed Mac down the stairs with Katherine in his arms.

By the grace of God, Mac was able to keep his footing as he grabbed the stair rail, tumbling down three steps of the steep wooden stairway.

"Have you lost your mind?!" Mac yelled at NMI, as a startled Katherine started whimpering into Mac's shoulder.

NMI looked deranged and totally unhinged on the top of the stairs. "I'm calling your mother. You must be drunk!"

"Let me get this straight. You just tried to push me and the baby down the stairs, so I must be drunk?"

NMI stormed away back to the bedroom. "I'm calling her."

"Go ahead, just stay away from me and Katherine," Mac said as he gathered himself and made his way down the rest of the stairway to the kitchen.

Mercifully, NMI stayed upstairs until Mac's mother, Searlait, made the ten-minute drive over from Fairmount to check on the situation.

Mac had opened the front entrance of the house and unlocked the storm door, awaiting the arrival of his mother as he continued to feed his daughter breakfast.

Searlait walked up the stoop to the house and quietly let herself into the large, white colonial home. Mac was almost done feeding Katherine in the highchair in the kitchen. He turned around and caught his mother's curious and worried glance.

Mac, standing in the middle of the kitchen with his rumpled shirt, tie, and dress pants, just shrugged and pointed with his chin upstairs. Katherine excitedly made baby noises to get her grandmother's attention.

"NMI?" Searlait called up the stairs from the foyer.

NMI came down the stairs in a huff: glaring at Mac in the kitchen, "Your son came home drunk after spending the night at some girl's house!"

Searlait looked back at Mac. "Patrick?"

"Mom, instead of spending a restless night yet again on the couch in the basement, I played cards at Mulrooney's with the guys. I'm neither drunk nor having an affair, but NMI already knows this."

"Whatever. You deal with this. I'm late for work." And with that, NMI grabbed her blue Coach purse off the stairs and rushed out of the house.

"Patrick, what's going on?" Searlait asked, as she picked up Katherine and sat in one of the kitchen chairs.

"Mom, as you know, NMI doesn't do anything to take care of me, the baby, or the house. She hasn't been affectionate to me since we agreed to have Katherine. It seems she just used me to get a nice house and have a baby. I'm just over it," Mac said, as he slumped into one of the other kitchen chairs.

"Have you tried counseling again?"

"She won't go back to counseling, Mom. The councilors told her last time it wasn't me. Remember? They said she had things to work on because her mother died young. She didn't follow through with that, so she won't go back."

"Well, this can't continue," Searlait said with a sigh, kissing Katherine on the forehead.

"You're right, but there's something else."

"What is it, Patrick?"

"I've been having chest pains."

"What?!"

"It's fine Mom. I went to the doctor, and they ran a stress test on me. I'm in perfect health. The doctor says I'm having panic attacks. It seems embarrassing, but it directly correlates with the issues with NMI."

"Oh, Patrick. I know you don't want to disappoint little Katherine here, but something has to be done sooner rather than later."

"I know Mom. I know."

There is no lonelier man in death, except the suicide, than that man who has lived many years with a good wife and then outlived her. If two people love each other there can be no happy end to it.

- Ernest Hemingway

CHAPTER TWENTY-NINE

Two weeks before Katherine's first birthday, Mac moved out of the house without notice. He rented a two-bedroom apartment at the Westwood, just five minutes down the road.

Mac took off his white gold wedding ring with the emerald and diamond chips, putting it on the top of his dresser in the master bedroom. He was hoping the symbolic gesture would be temporary and NMI would come back to her senses.

If she couldn't make the simplest effort to save the

marriage, why was he trying so hard to keep it alive?

Katherine was the answer, of course: but so was his eternal love for NMI.

But there was something else at play that had been going on for a very long time now. Neither Mac nor his little voice could ever have suspected what it actually ended up being. Earth shattering comes to mind though...

At the time, Mac surely thought that if left to her own devises, that NMI would make some grand gesture to have him return to the home. So, with a heavy heart, he decided he would walk out of his dream house, leaving his baby daughter, and the love of his life; hoping that he would be returning in a week or two.

After dinner that night, when he had the evening off from work, Mac went upstairs without a word and packed his clothes from the master bedroom.

NMI indubitably freaked out. "What are you doing?"

"I'm moving out. I've got a place at the Westwood Apartments. Building #5, apartment #202. You can drop Katherine off on the way to work, or I can come back and watch her in the morning until you get done. Just let me know which one you want me to do."

Mac's eyes glistened as he gave Katherine a kiss on the cheek and took his clothes to the unfurnished apartment. Shortly thereafter, NMI arrived at his apartment crying. She had brought Katherine to her father's house. "Why are you doing this?"

"You know why. Why have I been sleeping in the basement for almost two years? Why do I do all the housework? The yardwork? The groceries? The cooking? Why do I pay the mortgage and almost all the bills? Why don't you show any affection towards me?" Mac said through tears of his own.

NMI just stood there looking at him for a minute or two before walking back out of the apartment.

Mac slept on the floor that night and literally cried himself to sleep.

The next day he visited garage and yard sales, purchasing second-hand items to furnish the house. He did, however, splurge on new bedroom sets from Ashley Furniture for Katherine and himself.

In Mac's mind, this was just temporary, but he needed to have someplace nice for his daughter in the meantime. Even with the second-hand couch, television, kitchen table, and chairs; Mac made it work.

*

As if the universe itself knows that once one door closes, another one opens, Mac was promoted to sergeant for the City of Syracuse Police Department.

He was assigned to the Road Patrol Division on the Third Platoon; where coincidently he had started when he transferred from the Town of Camillus Police Department some fifteen years earlier.

The two shifts for the Third Platoon were either early (1400-2200) or late (1500-2300.)

Mac needed the late shift so he could still care for Katherine while NMI was at work.

The captain, lieutenant, the other sergeants, and rank-and-file cops were the best in the police department. Third Platoon was the busiest shift for call volume and violent crime. No one stayed on this shift for long if they couldn't hack it.

That was fine with Patrick MacKena. He always gravitated to where the action was, and this was the only place he could imagine himself as a frontline supervisor.

*

Shortly after the sergeant promotion at SPD, Mac was sent off to Wright-Patterson Air Force Base for his military annual two-week special agent training. He had continued to do Protective Service Operations in New York City and liked the work. Long as the hours were, he still admired the command staff officers he was protecting, as well as the special agents he worked with from Detachment 426.

Wright-Patterson Air Force Base, situated on the northeastern outskirts of Dayton, Ohio, is a significant military installation. The base is steeped in a rich aviation heritage, with historical aircraft displayed throughout. The groundbreaking work carried out by Orville and Wilbur Wright between 1899 and 1903 resulted in their historic achievement of the first-ever manned, powered flight.

Once they had accomplished their historic feat at Kitty Hawk, they headed back to Dayton, Ohio. In 1904 and 1905, they tirelessly labored to improve their flying abilities, simultaneously transforming the Wright Flyer into the first-ever functional aircraft that offered full control while airborne.

At the Huffman Prairie Flying Field, now incorporated into Wright-Patterson Air Force Base, they successfully completed this task. At Huffman Prairie, a flying school operated by the brothers thrived from 1910 to 1916, they attracted students eager to learn the secrets of flight.

As headquarters for a worldwide logistics system, a renowned research laboratory, and the leading center for acquisition and development in the US Air Force, the base is a pivotal location. Wright-Patterson is home to numerous associate organizations, representing a wide range of Air Force and Department of Defense activities. Imagine a base that offers everything from shopping facilities and child care centers to housing areas and a large medical center—it's like a medium-sized city in itself.

Major units at Wright-Patterson Air Force Base include the 88th Air Base Wing, Air Force Materiel Command, Air Force Life Cycle Management Center, Air Force Research Laboratory, National Air and Space Intelligence Center, 445th Airlift Wing, Air Force Institute of Technology, Air Force Installation Contracting Center, and the National Museum of the United States Air Force.

The Air Force Marathon is also held at Wright-Patterson Air Force Base on the third Saturday of September every year.

With its association with Project Blue Book, Wright-Patterson Air Force Base has gained a reputation for being a hotbed of UFO-related mysteries, putting it in the same league as Area 51.

Hangar 18, a building located within Wright-Patt, has become the center of speculation and intrigue, with numerous rumors circulating about the secretive happenings that occurred inside. The belief among UFO enthusiasts is that the government deliberately concealed tangible proof obtained during their investigations. Inside the highly secured confines of "the Blue Room," a mysterious warehouse, they claim to have hidden flying saucer fragments, extraterrestrial remains, and even captured aliens.

That being what it may be, Mac had a long trip ahead of him to contemplate the theories.

Appreciatively, Mac had just upgraded vehicles from the Saab to a 2001 BMW X5 Sport Activity Vehicle. It wasn't new, but it was roomy.

The eight-hour drive to Wright-Patterson was going to be grueling. Searlait had agreed to watch Katherine during the two-week training, which took a little off Mac's mind as he traveled west.

His little voice: "Maybe you'll get a chance to solve the riddle of Hangar 18?"

"Not very likely," Mac said through the windshield, as he had many other pressing concerns on his mind.

The trip went faster than he realized, and before

long, he was in classrooms conducting his annual training for the Air Force. Most of the exercises were computer-based. Updating the annual requirements in which Air Force personnel and special agents acknowledge certain rules and regulations that were required of them.

The Air Force Base was massive; the largest base he'd been on. There was a flurry of activity everywhere he looked.

However, Mac knew enough not to ask where Hangar 18 was located.

Firearms qualifications were always welcome. Mac qualified as a distinguished expert once again on the firing line.

Even though it wasn't required for the AT; Mac ran around the base just about every night keeping in shape for the annual physical fitness test which would be given on the last Friday of training. He was confident that he would have no issues passing it, but he always wanted to try for a personal record every time he took it.

Mac didn't know any of the special agents training

with him and kept to himself. He was trying to punch his ticket and get back to Camillus to see his daughter as quickly as he could. Bridget, Joseph, and Elizabeth were grown up and doing their own things, but he missed them just as much.

The final day in AT came with the physical battery test being executed at 0700 hours, just off one of the many flight lines on base.

Mac felt good physically, crushing the sit-ups, push-ups, and the agility run. The 1.5-mile run was next, and he was running at a sub-seven-minute pace when he started sprinting to the finish line. Just before he crossed it, he heard and felt a loud snap. Without warning, Mac's left ankle kicked out from under him. He scarcely kept his balance as he stumbled over the finish line. Crashing in a heap on the asphalt: holding his left ankle gingerly in his hands.

"What happened? The instructor inquired, running up to Mac.

"I, I don't know. Something just snapped."

"Can you walk?"

Mac tried to get up off the tarmac but couldn't.

"Okay, you stay right there, Patrick. I'll get some guys to help you get to the base hospital."

Mac just nodded, trying to keep the pain at bay, and not letting anyone know he was truly hurt.

*

"What do you mean, you have a torn Achilles?" The Senior Master Sergeant contact at OSI Andrews Air Force Base was asking Mac over the phone.

"Geez, I don't know. That's what the x-ray is showing them, but they can't be sure without further tests. What do you want me to do?" Mac asked. He had been placed in a soft cast with ace bandages wrapped all the way up his upper leg to his foot. Metal crutches were nearby.

"Well, your annual training wraps up today. Do you have health insurance through your civilian job?"

"Uh, yes. Blue Cross Blue Shield."

"Perfect. Drive yourself home and have your local

doctors treat it. Get back to us when they know what exactly it is."

"Really?" Mac asked, but the E-8 on the other end had already finished the phone conversation.

Driving eight hours on Hydrocodone didn't seem like a great idea, so Mac made the trip back sweating bullets through the pain.

He was pushing the top end speed of the BMW as he crossed into Buffalo, New York. Soon, red lights filled up his rearview mirror.

"You've got to be kidding me." He just wanted to get home and elevate his leg.

"Hey, Mac! Is that you?" A tall, imposing New York State Trooper asked, coming up to the open window of Mac's BMW.

"Uh, yeah," Mac answered in confusion, trying to look back over his shoulder at the unknown voice.

"It's Craig. I worked with you at the State Fair detail in Syracuse last fall."

"Oh shoot. Hi Craig...how have you been?"

"Apparently better than you," Craig said, adjusting his Stetson on top of his head. He had just spied the crutches in the backseat.

"Yeah, screwed up my Achilles at military training in Ohio. Sorry if I was going a little fast. Just trying to get home from drill."

"No worries. I'll call out ahead for you on the Thruway and let the guys and gals know you're coming. Get better...I'll see you at the next Fair!"

"Thanks!"

The Trooper's extremely nice gesture made Mac's leg ache just a little less as he put the car back in gear and continued his journey home.

Mac wasn't sure where his military career with AFOSI was going after what appeared to be a significant injury, but the sub-two-hour ride home to his empty apartment gave him some time to think about it.

Some of the most amazing people I've met
in life are cops.

- Omari Hardwick

CHAPTER THIRTY

As the winter season for 2005 began in earnest, Mac dragged himself through the sleet, hail, and snow in upstate New York from doctor's appointment to doctor's appointment trying to get a proper diagnosis for his ailing left ankle. He had previously broken the same ankle in the Central New York Police Academy some eighteen years prior, and then sprained it countless times playing basketball and box lacrosse over the years.

Finally, after stepping in a sewer grate behind the

Rescue Mission while chasing a wanted felon at SPD in his earlier years.: Mac was transported to the hospital by ambulance, where he eventually had total reconstruction surgery to tighten up the ligaments and tendons that kept on failing.

Now the orthopedic surgeon was telling Mac that he had an avulsion of the left Achilles, in which the tendon that attached to the bone on the very bottom of his left foot had been completely torn off. This would require surgery to reattach the tendon, drill a new hole into the bone in which to affix it, and six months of convalescing and physical therapy.

This created a whole new dilemma. Mac was still paying the full mortgage at the palace he was no longer living at, and the added expense of the two-bedroom apartment for him and his daughter.

There would be no more overtime coming in to supplement his base pay at the police department. No additional pay either from the Air Force for weekend drills—which seemed crazy, because this was the ultimate reason he was injured. Mac also would apparently burn through his sick time at SPD to cover the operation and recovery—which also didn't quite make sense to him since it was a military training evolution that was the reason he was out of work.

Mac recontacted the Senior Master Sergeant at AFOSI Andrews Air Base and relayed the information that he had received from the orthopedic surgeon.

"Great, let us know when you have a clean bill of health and we'll get you scheduled for your next drill," came the response from the E-8.

"But, doesn't the Air Force cover me for..."

It was too late. The Senior Master Sergeant had already hung up the call.

Mac's little voice: "Now you've really done it. No money coming in, no one to take care of you, and you still have to take care of a toddler on your own. Nice job, Patrick! What's next?"

He thought about it for a bit. Mac had always worked two to three jobs since he was nineteen years old. He just couldn't sit still and not be productive. Taking care of his daughter was essential for him, but he needed to find something else to do with his downtime.

Mac decided that continuing his education made perfectly good sense. He really couldn't do anything physical for a while, but he still could read and type on a computer. He thought about getting a Master's in Fine Arts, but after conferring with a retired SPD lieutenant who was the Chair of the Criminal Justice Department at Onondaga Community College; Mac decided he would enroll in a Master's of Science in Criminal Justice Degree at Columbia College—so he could adjunct at OCC in the future.

The MSCJ seemed redundant, but Mac was able to use the rest of his GI Bill to pay for the nearly ten-thousand-dollar graduate program, enrolling in night school for Columbia College at Hancock Air Field in Syracuse, New York.

The surgical procedure was still a month away.

In the meantime, he took care of Katherine during the day while NMI was at work. He kept her overnight in her new bedroom furniture two to three nights a week and started his new grad curriculum.

NMI showed no signs of remorse or regret about him moving out. The nights Katherine wasn't at the apartment were long and lonely. With nothing else to do on a wintery Thursday night, Mac decided to bundle up, grab his crutches, and head downtown to Mulrooney's for some adult conversation.

Parking as close as he could get to the Irish Bar, he carefully sticked his way with the crutches through the foot and a half of freshly fallen snow to the warm ambiance of the festive tavern.

He was delighted to see his son Joseph at the door as he made his entrance just shortly after 2300 hours. Joseph hadn't returned to Utica College and was living with a friend as he continued working at Mully's as a bouncer and sometimes barback. Joseph, now twenty-two years of age, was just over 6'2" tall and skinny as a fence post. He had grown out his light brown hair, and it was tied up in a neat ponytail for the evening night's work.

"Hey, Dad! How's the ankle?" Joseph said, giving his father a warm embrace.

"Same. Unfortunately, it won't get better until I have surgery next month. Can you take me to the clinic for the procedure?"

"Sure Dad, just let me know what day and time," Joseph said, smiling.

Joseph Mackenna was wearing the winter Mully's uniform of a white dress shirt, with the Mulrooney family crest and the embroidered logo of BE GOOD OR BE GONE, a red dress tie tucked in, blue jeans, and brown Timberland work boots.

Mac had to step out of the foyer so Joseph could ID the group of Lemoyne College students who had shown up to get in. Joseph turned towards them and held up his forefinger and thumb to the kids, signaling that he needed to see a driver's license to enter the bar.

Walking on the crutches to the back bar, Mac found Danny, the bartender, slinging drinks to the youthful crowd. Danny was dressed similarly to his son.

"What's the good word Mac?"

"Still waiting on getting this fixed," Mac said, putting his crutches against the back wall and raising his left leg.

"Well, let's see if I can help you with some pain management then," Danny winked, picking up a pint glass and making a Captain Morgan and Diet Coke with a wedge of lime placed on the rim.

"Thank you, my friend." Mac raised the glass and took a sip. "Kind of busy tonight, isn't it?"

"Yeah, the Lemoyne lacrosse team is having some type of soiree here tonight."

Danny was a Lemoyne College alumnus himself. Being from the Albany, New York area, he had drunk and then worked at Mulrooney's and never left.

Mac stood like a flamingo in the corner of the back bar, people-watching and occasionally talking to Danny through the number of libations he was making as the night ticked on until the nearly 0200 hours closing time.

Then the trouble started.

Joseph was at the side door, refusing entry to a large crowd that wanted to come into the establishment. Last Call had already been given, and no one was allowed in after that edict.

The back bar had cleared out where Mac and Danny were mildly paying attention to the routine disagreement when one of the guys pulled a can of mace and sprayed Joseph in the face.

Mac forgot about the injury to his left ankle, hopscotching his way to the front door before Danny had time to jump the bar. Joseph, temporarily blinded by the mace, backed out of the entryway and into the bar as the ten young males passed into the tavern.

He got there just as the main aggressor with the mace was a couple of feet inside. Mac could then recognize the group as the Eastwood Gang from the north side of the city. They were a bunch of white trash lowlifes who sold drugs and were engaged in gang assaults across the city and county.

The leader with the mace most likely didn't recognize Mac as a cop, or the newly minted SPD sergeant that he was, nor that it was his son who had just gotten maced, but the look in Mac's eyes froze that gang banger solid in his tracks, as he observed a large oddity hopping his way with a full head of steam.

Mac grabbed the miscreant by his coat collar, propelling him backward and crashing into the awaiting rest of the gang and the nighttime city street. The front bartender, Double D, Flower the bar back, and two other bouncers came through the door into the throng with Danny, as Mac found a parked car on the side of the street and started laying into the shorter and smaller gang banger with both fists. The mace can the wrongdoer was carrying fell harmlessly into the snowbank.

Patrick MacKenna rarely lost his temper, but was seeing red and wouldn't be dissuaded from his current task at hand during this juncture. In the frosty air and without the benefit of a coat, Mac was free to throw fist to face successfully time after time. It was only after a brief thought that this fight was going way too easy that he started feeling sustaining blows in the back of the head by two unseen assailants.

The beating he was taking was unsustainable. Every time Mac delivered a punch to the assailant, he took two blows to the back of his head from the pair of gang bangers behind him. His knees buckled after every hit, but he was determined to stay in the fight and hold the third man against the parked car and keep swinging.

Adding to the complexity of the situation, Mac's left

foot was tightly wrapped up in ace bandages. Not long ago, he was gripping his steel crutches, feeling the cold metal against his palms as he moved around the Armory Square business district in downtown Syracuse.

Initially, the third man Mac was engaged with had attacked him fiercely. Now, however, he was content to just parry Mac's strikes and let his allies on the back side do their worst.

As the melee raged on, Mac felt a cold snowflake land on his eyelash, its crystalline beauty standing out amongst the chaos. He could sense it melting, as dark clouds in his head swirled and his legs continued to rachet his body down into the cold slushy snow beneath him in the street. The punches from behind kept coming as Mac was being dragged away from the present...

Just in time, Danny and Double D engaged the two blindside snipers who were getting the best of Mac. Shaking his head to clear the cobwebs, Mac took the gang leader to the snow-filled street and straddled his chest, effectively pinning him to the ground and preventing escape.

The fight raged on in the wintery street as the wind

pushed swirls of fallen snow around the pugilistic menagerie of foes. Which would've seemed almost whimsical, save for the bloody droplets that added a colorful yet darker scenario to the actions in the roadway.

Joseph had recovered and had entered into the fray to apprehend one of the violators as well. All told, even though professional bad guys outnumbered the Mully's crew, seven of the ten were detained by the time marked units of the Syracuse Police Department made it to the scene. One of the remaining Lemoyne College patrons had called 911 and reported the large disturbance which brought the cavalry.

One by one, the Eastwood Gang was loaded into the back of the Paddy Wagon. Once all corralled, a uniform midnight patrol officer helped Mac onto the back of the truck and said, "Hey Sarge, what are we charging these mopes with anyhow?"

The lumped-up gang bangers mouths slightly dropped open upon the realization of Mac being an SPD sergeant, "Gang Assault, Criminal Trespass, and Criminal Possession of a Noxious Material. Place a hold on them for the night."

"Will do Sarge. You need any help getting back to Mulroney's?"

"No, I got it. Thanks." Mac said, as he gingerly came down off the back of the truck, making his way through the snowy street back to the warmth of Mully's to regain his crutches.

It turned out that the Eastwood Gang had been slighted in some way by the Lemoyne lacrosse team at another bar nicknamed the Shire, and they had showed up at Mulrooney's to settle the score with an overpowering brawl inside the bar.

Mac was grateful that he had been there that night for his son, Joseph. The ankle was a little worse than when he first started out for the evening, but a torn Achilles was a torn Achilles at the end of the day. Next month's surgery would hopefully rectify that.

A lot had transpired for Mac in the preceding four years. He was looking forward to what his role as a supervisor for the City of Syracuse Police Department would offer him in the future.

Stay tuned...

It does not matter how slowly you go as long as you do not stop.

\- Confucius

EPILOGUE

"**Bang!**"

The loud report echoing somewhere within the Armory Square district of downtown Syracuse had punctuated the early spring, late-night stillness.

The fickle Central New York weather conditions had given its residents what had promises of even a better climate just around the corner.

Patrick Mackenna was taking advantage of the gift by Mother Nature wearing a teal Henley long-sleeve

Banana Republic shirt, tan J. Crew cargo shorts, and a Murphy & Johnston tan sandal on his bare-toed right foot. He had his ever-present blued Boston Red Sox cap covering his head, and a recently acquired purple walking cast worn up to his knee on his left leg.

On this very exceptionally nocturnal early morning, he was sitting at an outdoor table in the fenced-in courtyard of the latest nightclub in the entertainment zone of the city. Daisy Dukes had just opened in March 2005. The country-themed nightclub based on the old television show, Dukes of Hazard, was appropriately decorated with the all-female bar staff wearing cutoff denim shorts and red and white checkered button shirts tied at the waist, complete with cowboy boots.

Not too long ago, Flower had been a bar back and bartender at Mulrooney's, but was now the general manager for the new haunt in the Armory.

Being a Thursday night, the crowds were thin in the square and faint music could be heard from the fellow establishments in the calm seasonal air that flowed between the other bars and late-night restaurants.

Mac had been brought out of his hibernation and

studying in his apartment by one of his old mates from the Criminal Investigations Division at the Syracuse Police Department. Liam Fletcher, who had worked that night in CID, but had just left the table that Mac now occupied, his empty Bud Light beer bottle still sitting on top of the black iron framed table.

He had heard the loud noise, but had written it off as some assclown setting off a single firecracker somewhere within the business district.

Mac was finishing up his Captain Morgan and Diet Coke when a bulky bouncer in an overly tight Daisy Dukes black t-shirt - stenciled on the back with large white lettering STAFF - came over to his table.

"Hey, aren't you a cop?"

Not being familiar with the bouncer, Mac looked around to make sure he was the one being addressed. Looking back at the goliath he said, "Uh, yeah."

"Well, this dude just shot this guy outside the gate by the pizza place."

Instinctively, Mac reached to his right side to feel for the firearm, which wasn't there. Since he had ripped his Achilles tendon, he hadn't been carrying it. Mac didn't think he'd be playing cop on one leg.

He stood up with some assistance from the table to help get his weight underneath his bad leg. "Where?"

The bouncer started walking outside the gate, turning left, as Mac hobbled on after him. After about ten yards, the doorman pointed to a young white male who was lying on the side of the street face up. His eyes were fluttering back up at Mac and the bouncer as a small crowd appeared around the body.

Taking this all in, Mac's assessment was interrupted when the Daisy Duke employee said, "And there's the guy that shot him!"

Following the finger of the bouncer, Mac saw a late twenties white male across the street on top of the cement stairs of another restaurant thirty yards away. He glanced back at the victim and back to the suspect, deciding that the suspect was still an imminent danger, and forewent any lifesaving procedures on the man supine in the street.

In somewhat of a fugue, Mac started hobbling

towards the suspect before he had made a firm mental plan on how he was going to apprehend the felon. Thankfully, he had only had the proverbial two drinks before all this unfolded.

Before he knew it, his little voice was taking control of the situation, “Blend in with the crowd until you’re right on top of him. Then take him into custody before he gets a chance to pull his gun again.”

Now usually Mac would debate his inner voice, but this actually seemed like a good plan.

As he continued in the suspect's direction, the crowd that Mac was trying to blend in with must have sensed what was emerging in front of them, causing them to scatter like cats in all directions, leaving Mac in the middle of Walton Street still advancing on the gunman on the steps.

“Not really a great plan!” Mac mentally scolded his little voice.

“Oops!” was the only reply he got from his conscience.

But Mac kept on limping in his progress towards his

target. Really, what else was there to do?

He was still a sergeant for SPD, even though unarmed, out of work because of injury, but retreat in this kind of situation was never really covered at the academy.

When Mac was way too close, the gunman realized what was happening and started reaching frantically into the right front pants pocket of his jeans...

With no other options, Mac stopped his advance. Reaching into the left back pocket of his cargo shorts; he produced his shiny new gold sergeant's badge, showing this to his target. He simultaneously reached into his empty front pants pocket with his right hand as if he were reaching for his own gun.

"Syracuse Police...Freeze!"

Time stood still as the fifty or so onlookers held their collective breaths, waiting on the next move in the faceoff at Armory Square...

Thanks for reading! Please add a short review and let me know what you thought!

— *Murph*

About the Author

Dennis Patrick Murphy, MSCJ, is a Navy veteran, former United States Air Force Reserve-OSI agent, and adjunct professor who attained a graduate degree in Criminal Justice and has held the following titles in law enforcement and the military over his thirty-six-year career: Police Officer, ERT Operator, Detective, DEA Task Force Agent, Police Sergeant, Detective Sergeant, Police Lieutenant, Detective Lieutenant, Supervising Criminal Investigator, Senior Federal Investigator, Law Enforcement Coordinator, Intelligence Specialist, Operational Representative, and Special Agent. However, his favorite title is "Dad" to his four children.

DENNIS PATRICK
Murphy